TARANTULA WOMAN

Donald O'Donovan

Published by Open Books 2011

Cover art "India" by Jacqui Simpson
Learn more about the artist at riffo.deviantart.com

ISBN: 0615722849
ISBN-13: 978-0615722849

1

AS A CHILD I WAS A TAOIST. Then I departed from the Way. It wasn't my decision. I was forced, by secret urges and demonic voices in the blood. The decision to leave the Garden originated in the germplasm, in the liver, in the spleen. In the pituitary, if you will. Or in the pancreas. It was a matter of chemistry.

Once I was the joyful inhabitant of a tiny, ordered world whose enameled blue sky my extended fingers could always touch. Then the serpent entered the Garden. The enzymes were released. My eyes were opened. And so it began: cities, women, occupations. In other words, my life...

It was right after I was rejected by the Peace Corps, when I was living in El Paso, that I started writing letters for the girls across the river, in Ciudad Juárez—the girls of Mariscal Street—the butterflies who inhabited the Boulevard of Broken Dreams.

I wanted to be a writer and I figured that a writer should write. Simple, no? The letter-writing practice I set up on *La Calle Mariscal* paid off chiefly in meals, drinks, and an occasional fuck—with the meter running, of course. Like Fallopio the Traveling Abortionist, I trekked from cantina to cantina, dispensing my services. The butterflies of Mariscal Street wanted letters written in English, letters to their customers and boyfriends, letters to their sugar daddies in *Los Estados Unidos*, letters to soldiers, sailors and airmen all over the world. They'd tell me in Spanish; I wrote in English. Looking back, I'm amazed at the gush and goo I copied down or translated or transliterated. At the lies I told or may have told, quite inadvertently. At the tragedies I may have precipitated with a mistaken phrase or two. Please understand, my Spanish wasn't all that good.

The Navy Rose Club was home to me. Above the swinging doors was a sign, "La Rosa Marina, Navy Rose Club," and a cracked, weathered ship's figurehead, a hatchet faced maiden with an unswerving gaze and seaweed tangled in her long streaming hair. The Durango Club next door, somewhat upscale, featured a neon scorpion with a madly flagellating tail, as well as a midget doorman named Paco. "*How-do-you-do-my-friend-take-a-look-inside!*" he'd chirp, swinging the door open with a flourish. These were the only words of English he knew.

One of my best clients worked at the Navy Rose, Profunda, a broad-beamed woman with a nose like the blade of an oar. It had been broken several times. Her eyes were a little out of kilter, too. She was dewy, sentimental, highly sexed. She melted at the touch of a finger. Profunda was large and unwieldy, more than six feet tall. She towered above me. I felt like a rubber duck in her hands. She wanted the last drop of juice, everything. At the same time, she was terrified of getting pregnant. She took elaborate precautions.

"*Estoy buscando un marido,*" she told me frankly one afternoon in bed. "*Me entiendes?* I am looking for a father for my *bebés.*"

I wrote many letters for Profunda to a one-armed retired colonel in Santa Monica who was constantly begging her to marry him. The Colonel was past sixty, an ex-paratrooper who raised roses and Great Danes. He was wiry and rugged, a little below medium height. His grizzled chest hair poked out of the brilliant Hawaiian shirts he always wore. The Colonel had a steel plate in his head and an eye that watered constantly. The left side of his face, which featured the weeping banjo eye, had been disfigured by a shrapnel burst. He was a tough little stud, a regular iron man, a booze artist, and horny as a monkey. What the Colonel desperately needed was a sea anchor, a doting wife for his declining years. He was in love with Profunda, as his frequent visits and many letters amply testified.

The visits of Profunda's one-armed chicken colonel from Santa Monica were spectacular events. The rug was rolled out at the Navy Rose Club. There was a tremendous upsurge in morale among the personnel. Profunda was hot. Profunda was everybody's Cinderella. Her *compadres* huddled around her, nudging, pushing, patting. Everyone wanted to see Cinderella get her Prince.

When the little iron man departed, things were quiet for a while. Then the influx of letters began. This is where I came in. In the afternoons, after a vigorous tumble in the hay, Profunda would sit in the chair by the window, putting on her makeup. She was getting ready to go to work. It was a long, drawn-out process, and she took her time. I'd sit on the edge of the bed with the night stand pulled up to my knees, writing to the Colonel. *"Dear Ralph..."* Profunda liked to dictate her letters to the Colonel when she was freshly fucked. After several orgasms she became light and buoyant. She was a garden that had been plowed and tilled and fertilized, and now she was blooming. Her talk flowed. I had to keep stopping her. All the while she was preparing herself for the upcoming night's work like a gladiator getting ready for a bout in the arena. Often I forgot to write as I watched her apply the lavish eye shadow, the butterfly lashes, the arched eyebrows boldly sketched with crude slashes of mascara. Profunda's face could have been stamped on a Roman coin: the strong masculine nose, the rounded resolute chin blending into heavy jowls that bristled with sparse black hairs, and the full lips that glistened with a kissy-wet sheen. Her big knockers, warm, perfumed, swaying inside her robe, bulged with branching blue veins.

As I resumed my scribbling, I thought about the chicken colonel from Santa Monica, this furry-chested goat-god with cloven hooves of iron. He'd have to be made of iron, by Jesus, to take care of a woman like Profunda. Could he do it? Profunda was a hulking, steaming locomotive of a woman. Was this little soldier man enough to tend the fire in her boiler?

"Listen, soldier," I said to him, rapping the dusty toe of his boot with my swagger stick. "Stand up straight when I talk to you! Listen, you little iron man. I'm making you a gift of her, see? I'm giving you a field to be plowed and fertilized, a bed of live coals that needs to be stirred vigorously and often. This here is a locomotive-woman. She needs her ashes hauled. Listen, you bugger. This is a WOMAN. You're sticking your iron poker into a raging furnace of love, do you realize that?"

For Profunda, it was a chance in a million. All she had to do, as the Beauty, was surrender herself to the Beast, and her life would be transformed. In a matter of days, if she said the word, she'd be driving a Lincoln Continental, shopping at Nordstrom's, lazing in a heated pool. Her *niños* would have a splendid patrimony. They would be Americans. Why, then, did she drag her heels?

Because, she insisted, she was in love with *me*.

Profunda had a crush on me and I couldn't handle it. That was the basis of our relationship. Profunda came from *Calle O* in Colonia Alta Vista, a dirt street where people lived like animals in mud huts without electricity or running water. Several times I went home with her and we had dinner with the parents. I was astonished at their diminutive size. How could these tiny *Indios*, little stick-figures like the *penitentes* I'd seen crawling in the aisles of the Basilica of Guadalupe in Mexico City, have given birth to a giantess, a Neolithic princess like Profunda? Each time I visited, they insisted on giving me the bed while they slept on the floor of the hut with Profunda and Profunda's "*bebés*," three lusty half-American infants.

We'd go to the *cine*, Profunda and I. Just pals, no romance. Then one night in a theater she unzipped my fly and made me come while we watched some stupid Japanese monster movie with subtitles *en Español*. After that we sort of lived together, mostly in her cell at the Navy Rose Club. We talked about a hair dryer. She got the literature on the damn thing. It cost $14.99. That hair dryer became an obsession, an albatross around my neck. I wanted to buy it for her, but I couldn't get the fifteen bucks together. Then I started feeling guilty. Profunda was falling in love with me, I could tell, and it was merely lust and convenience that brought me to her door.

Always on her lips was a phrase, repeated a dozen times a day, a phrase that was both a command and a plaintive question: "*Casate conmigo, corazón.* Why do you not wish to marry with me?"

Miguel Angel "Angel Mike," the bartender at the Navy Rose, was dark, astonishingly handsome and brimming over with *machismo*. The girls were crazy about him. He was a strong man, a real athlete, especially good at rousting belligerent drunks with his billy club, a sawed-off broomstick with a hole drilled in the end and the keys to the door and the register attached. Sometimes when things were slow, we'd arm wrestle. Usually I won, but it was tough going. Angel Mike was a real hombre, and a great *compadre*.

Another of my letter-writing clients was Sandra, a frantic fucking filly who had worked at the *Viejo Oeste*, the Old West Club, before joining the crew at the Navy Rose. The Old West Club, like the Durango, was somewhat ritzy, and the lopsided doorman stationed in front was sometimes good for a small loan.

Sandra's body was a wonder to behold. She couldn't

have weighed more than ninety pounds. Her arms and legs were like pipestems. And that luxurious black tuft of hair. It reminded me of a gorgeous, hot-blooded little forest creature, a sable or an ermine. It glared back at you, defiantly, mischievously, invitingly. I never saw another pussy quite like it.

Sandra would get wildly drunk. She'd fly into a rage, first jokingly, mockingly, then stubbornly she'd persist. She scratched, bit, clawed. She'd top off her tantrum with a crying session. First she got maudlin drunk, and then comically maudlin drunk, laughing at herself through her tears, very much the little girl in such moments. To "go to the room," with Sandra when she was in the throes of one of those moods was an unforgettable experience.

I adored Sandra and I spent many evenings buying drinks and mushing it up in the booth with her—she was free with affection—but I'd never been romantically in love with her as my friend Roscoe Longworth had. Sandra was sexy and a good pal and that was that. I wrote several letters for Sandra, in fact, to an undertaker in Trenton, New Jersey. But Roscoe had fallen hard for her on their first meeting, and then she dumped him. He gave her a ring—it was nothing, of course, a trinket he'd probably filched from a dimestore. But Sandra had a roomful of rings. And not only rings, but bracelets, lockets, necklaces, dolls, dried flowers and favors of all kinds. Once when I spent the night with her, we passed the next morning looking through her photographs, many of them snapped by strolling photographers in the Navy Rose Club with her client of the moment, but just as many of which had come enclosed in moistly ardent love letters mailed from cities all over the world. It was an army of men, studs, hard-legs, swinging dicks, soldiers and sailors of all nationalities, truck drivers, merchant seamen, cowboys and doddering oldsters promising her the moon. As I sat in Sandra's rickety chair in front of her dressing table mirror, sorting through these mementos, I felt myself as one of a teeming host, a single sperm cell among flagellating millions or billions swimming against the current with valiant flips and flails of their whippet-like tails, tiny semaphores winking in the fallopian darkness of Sandra's womb.

But Sandra—her fulfillment, I conjectured, required a handsome, almost unattainable man who would treat her cruelly and then abandon her. But when she eventually landed a well-to-do American, a retired judge from Wisconsin—an American Cheese, you might say—I wasn't in the least surprised. Sandra got her papers and went off to the US of A. After two months she was back, of her own accord, so she claimed, and although this was bitterly contested by both the girls at the Navy Rose and Sandra's old pals at the Viejo Oeste, who insisted that the papers were fake and the marriage was fake and that Sandra had been deported, I believed her story. Maybe Sandra had found that life with her American Cheese was unspeakably bland, who can say?

Any way you looked at her, Sandra was a wonderful girl, if a bit on the spiteful side. She had plenty of nerve. I loved her flashing white teeth, her tough-guy way of blowing the ashes off her cigarette, and when she wore her frilly red dress—the crinoline—her little knobby knees. I loved her husky tequila voice, very much like Edith Piaf's voice. Sandra had a heroic way of insisting on happiness; she *willed* happiness, like Grushenka. I adored Sandra aesthetically as well as personally and sexually. I never tired of gazing at her face, the arched eyebrows, the high cheekbones, the dimples at the corners of her wide mouth. I loved the defiant flare of her nostrils and her downy little mustache. But most of all I loved Sandra because she had the verve and the spirit to put on misfortune like a suit of armor and fling her whoredom in the teeth of the world.

Sandra's cohort, Viridiana, was the opposite. A lazy, slatternly slut. Viridiana smelled like a fish market. When it came time to go to the room she'd hit her customer up for a dinner. She took the plates to bed with her. She liked to get half undressed before pitching into her food. Viridiana had a beautiful body, but somehow one was disappointed because...there was nobody home. It was like crawling on top of a big, beautiful, bouncy rubber dolly, the kind Swedish sailors take with them on long voyages.

Viridiana was like a sea cow in a lazy, sloppy way. A slob is what she was. Always there were saucers, crumbs, forks and sticky coffee spoons and scraps of food in her bed. She was dirty. She wiped her shoes on the bed sheets, and I suspected her ass as well.

When Viridiana got drunk she became abusive. She'd beg for coins in an aggressive mock-humble fashion. When she was very drunk she waxed homicidal. One night she sliced a German soldier's face open with a broken beer bottle. Always she was turning up with a black eye, and frequently her body was covered with bruises. She got in fights, whore-fights, knockdown, drag-out, hair-pulling tussles that ended up with the combatants rolling on the dance floor and the *federales* hustling in—and hustling them *out*—the door. The other girls at the Navy Rose, except Sandra, gave Viridiana a wide berth. Hexed-up is what she was. Her eyes, when you looked into them, never seemed to be connected to the brain that was yelling red murder behind them. Her whole being was a clumsy protest, a strangled cry of rage at life for using her as it had. When she was completely sozzled, it was incoherent anger that came out, and finally dumb tears. But there was no intelligence in her outpourings, no flair, as with Sandra. It was a very different thing.

Viridiana had a perfect white scar on her left breast, the result of a knife-fight in Matamoros. The scar contrasted in its perfection and neatness Viridiana's slovenly personality: three dots on either side of a vertical line, a perfect six of dominoes. The scar added immeasurably to the attractiveness of the breast. In fact, with the passage of time, as Viridiana's body lost its allure for me, I came to think of her, or I should say I preferred to think of her, rather than contemplate her in her entirety, as just that—the scarred breast, that one rubbery sea-cow breast of hers, the Six of Dominoes.

Viridiana had a way of spoiling a hard-on, which was no less malicious on her part for being unconscious. Many nights in the room sitting beside me on the edge of the bed with her plate of food on her lap, she poured it out, bleary drunken talk, skirting the edge of tears, words humming with garlic, her breath stinging my eyes as I tried desperately, by staring at the scarred breast, to maintain some semblance of an erotic mood. When she finished talking she'd toss her plate on the floor and flop back on the bed with her legs up, weeping in a silly sea cow-like way with her mouth stuffed full of rice and beans.

One night I got a jolt that sobered me up in a split second. I was walking behind Viridiana in a jolly drunken lecherous mood, having just handed her my four bucks, squeezing her, playing grab-ass, anticipating, feeling her up; and on entering the room I saw by the flickering light of the saint's candle what looked for all the world like a bloody chunk of afterbirth on her pillow. It was an enchilada.

The afternoon bartender at the Navy Rose Club, Paulo, a close friend of mine, was a tall somber man with pitted skin. His face expressed melancholy enlivened by lust. Paulo had spent nine years in America as an illegal alien. He'd been a dancer in LA and New York. He wasn't famous, but he lived an exciting and glamorous life, an artistic life. Then one day it ended. He was apprehended and deported. His career was terminated, and he had to leave his male lover in New York. Now Paulo was back on the mean streets of his boyhood, a bartender in a whorehouse, middle-aged, his dancer's legs creaking as he trudged to the tables balancing a tray of drinks. Paulo was a kind person, gentle, generous, always ready with a tequila on the house, a small loan, or the price of a meal. He had a woman's voice, a perfect soprano.

Paulo's dreary existence at the Navy Rose Club was made bearable primarily by the daily visits of his sometime *amor* and constant confidant, Reymundo.

The word "fairy" was made for Reymundo. He was an ephemeral creature, a delicate flower, a mayfly perpetually poised for flight. He was a *peinadora*, a hairdresser. His shop was only a few doors away from the Navy Rose Club. All the girls had their hair done at Reymundo's place. Reymundo's own coiffure was also beautifully modeled. He wore rouge and mascara and frequently dressed as a woman. He traipsed through the red-light quarter, especially on soldiers' payday, wearing a sheath-like skirt wrapped tight around his hips, sparkling with a sheen of fish scales, and a sequined velveteen red blouse draped with a serape—a mantilla, rather—all lacy-like.

He darted into bars, he flitted here and there, twisting his curls, with a word, a pat, a seductive glance, a meaningful nod for this one and that, feverishly excited yet graceful as a butterfly. He knew everyone. He swished through the streets, whirling the *Nijinski-Scherezade*, frequently bursting into song, deliberately ogling the young soldiers, his hot brown eyes sparkling with frank open lust. A vein pulsed in his temple, another in his throat. Reymundo was all animal grace and hot-blooded vigor. Passion was everything to this creature. It was never money he was seeking, but love.

Sometimes, in the cantinas, after a tiff with one of his soldier boys, Reymundo hired the mariachis to play while he sang, pouring out his anguish. This was Reymundo's moment of triumph, belting out *ranchera* songs in his sweet tenor voice and weeping at the same time, while the street musicians sawed away at their violins. He emoted freely, without the least sense of shame.

Once I saw Reymundo pausing in front of a shop window, gazing pensively at his reflection. The store was a *carnicería*, a butcher shop. Behind the thick plate glass, which shimmered with the reflected glow of fizzing neon lights, a man in a blood-spattered apron hacked at a slab of red meat dangling from an iron hook. Reymundo didn't see the butcher; his gaze was fixed on the iridescent surface of the glass, on his own gossamer image. He dug in his purse and applied a jot of mascara to an eyelash, and then he sighed deeply and painted his generous mouth with more lipstick. Reymundo was a beautiful woman.

2

ONE MORNING I WENT TO SEE SANDRA at the Navy Rose Club. I'd heard through the grapevine that she wanted me to write a letter to the undertaker in Trenton. But Sandra wasn't in her room, and Paulo, behind the bar, told me that she'd gone across the street to Reymundo's *salon de belleza*. So I popped over there, and what a stink! I've never liked the smell of beauty parlors. It's as if the girls have to go through some kind of horrendous chemical torture in order to make them beautiful.

Sandra and Viridiana, waiting patiently, were reading movie magazines and Doctor Corazón comic books, while Reymundo combed out Profunda's hair. Sandra was a little drunk. She gave me a big smile then returned to her conversation.

"How is your *novio*, Viridiana?"

"Which one?"

"The Pepsi truck driver. From *Los Estados Unidos*."

"He don't come around no more."

"*Por qué no?* Why he don't come to see you, *mi amiga?*"

"I don't know. Could be he's in the slam."

"*Bueno*," Profunda put in. "I never liked him anyway."

"Yeah," Reymundo added. "He was a piece of shit."

"Maybe he's dead."

"I hope so. *Pinche guey!*"

And on and on like that, a bunch of half-witted cows chewing the cud. I wasn't surprised to learn that Viridiana's Pepsi truck driver had abandoned her—not because she was such a slob but because Pepsi is huge in Mexico and Pepsi drivers have money to burn, and of course the girls are gaga over those sexy uniforms with the Pepsi logo. The Pepsi drivers do all right for themselves in the cantinas, take it from me.

Reymundo put the finishing touches on Profunda's hair and held up a mirror.

"Ay, *mi amor!* You're the best," Profunda exclaimed. "You've made me beautiful!"

Just then the bells on the door jangled and my pal Roscoe Longworth walked in. He and Sandra exchanged icy glances as Roscoe climbed into the chair. Roscoe, by this time, had married a girl named Pilar, a real sourpuss he'd met at the Navy Rose, and they were living in El Paso. But being married to Pilar hadn't slowed Roscoe down one bit when it came to the honeys in the cantinas.

"Jerzy!" he began. "I'm glad I ran in to you, bro. I've got some news, big news."

It turned out that he'd just met a new girl, Minga, at a club called the Luz de Luna. He wanted to get spiffed up, and Reymundo had promised to give him a free haircut.

Minga was supposedly from Peru,

"Minga, the Peruvian Pelvis!" Roscoe quipped airily, addressing the room as Reymundo began to ply the scissors. "Wait till you meet her."

Sandra, a close friend of Pilar's, gave Roscoe a disgusted look and spat on the floor. "*Pinche Inglés, cabrón, malcriado!*"

Roscoe Longworth was a hooligan and a master of the gratuitous act. He liked to get bloody drunk and take savage deliberate pratfalls at the roller rink, even though he was an excellent skater. He'd also execute a pratfall in a cafeteria while carrying a tray loaded with food, sometimes knocking over tables or crashing into a dessert cart, creating a tremendous din. He'd get up brushing gravy and mashed potatoes and whipped cream off his pants, still playing it straight; he'd pretend to be mortified while everyone gawked, then he'd make for the door where he'd pause and do a tricky little dance step, then he'd let out a fusillade of braying laughter, grimacing horribly and rolling his eyes which glittered with indescribable mockery. The effect on the diners was devastating. Their reality was shattered. They couldn't believe—they refused to believe—that what they'd seen wasn't an accident. With the double takes, uncertain glances and suppressed hysterical laughter, it added up to a hair-raising performance—on the part of the audience. Their uncertainty was monumental. They didn't know whether to laugh or be indignant. They were caught off guard, and it was interesting to see them naked, as it were. The fragile icing of personality had cracked, revealing for a few hallucinating seconds the raw sticky dough underneath.

Why did Roscoe do these things? For the same reason that another man might paint a picture or commit a murder or write a book. His sense of insignificance was so overwhelming that he would do anything to rectify it.

Roscoe had a favorite book, *The Decay of the Angel* by Yukio Mishima. He carried it with him everywhere. The back cover of the book featured a photo of Mishima in a fierce Samurai pose—muscular torso, headband, sword. Though not an intellectual, Roscoe thoroughly embraced Mishima's doctrine of cosmic nihilism.

"Mishima wrote the last words of *The Decay of the Angel* on the day he killed himself," Roscoe was fond of saying. "*Seppuku*...ritual disembowelment."

Roscoe was ruled by his prick. With Roscoe it was a meal, a bottle, and a woman, in that order. Then, after a snooze, another meal, another bottle, another woman, and so on. That was his rhythm. As soon as he got a meal safely stowed away in his belly and a drink under his belt, his cock began to twitch like a snake. It never failed. The snake had a mind of its own. Once the thing began nosing around, Roscoe Longworth was helpless. Wherever the snake crawled or crept or slithered, wherever it led him, he followed: to bars, to brothels, down alleys, up fire escapes, through open windows. Roscoe Longworth was a snake with a man attached, and the snake was forever crawling, creeping, slithering. Searching, preferably, for something choice, fresh, moist, fleecy—something fragrant, something fringed with ermine. But in the event—as was usually the case—that there was nothing fresh and fleecy and fringed with ermine to be found, then the snake would gladly settle for something not so fragrant, like a can of worms, or a bucket of chopped chicken livers, a castrated rooster, a grease spot in the road, a dry hole in the wall, *anything.*

Once the chase was over, Roscoe was invariably dejected. He would whine like a flaccid prick. As soon as he got a meal, however, he took heart. His sinews began to stiffen. The blood rushed to his brain. A few slugs of firewater to grease the trolley and he was off, or rather the snake was off, off and slithering, on the prowl, delving and digging everywhere with its ugly spade-shaped head for some cozy fleece-lined nest where it could crawl inside and puke. It pissed Roscoe off, but that was his life; he hated himself, but he was helpless. His whole being was at the disposal of his cock. In his deflated stage, after a quick go in the back of some cantina, he was fond of declaring bitterly over the rim of his glass: "You come out of one dirty hole and after it's all over you end up in another dirty hole—like a hole in the fucking ground, get it? You come out of a hole and you spend your life trying to crawl back into that hole, that same goddamn hole, or one just like it. *Think about it!* But you never get back into that first hole, not all the way. *But that's what we're trying to do.* You know something? While the shits are nailing down the lid of my coffin, I'll probably still be jacking off. But...*Christ!* What else is there? Can you tell me? Yeah, that's what life is, all right. *A hole.* It's...nothing. Nothing! It's *nada*, that's what it is. *La vida no vale nada.*"

After Reymundo finished Roscoe's haircut, Sandra took his place in the chair. I figured it would be another hour, so Roscoe and I repaired to the Durango Club for drinks and more of Roscoe's excited blabbing about Minga, the Peruvian Pelvis. Then I joined Sandra in her room. She was pretty blitzed by now, sitting up naked in bed with a sheet pulled around her and nipping at a half empty a bottle of tequila. I sat in a chair next to the bed with a yellow legal pad in my lap. I was more than a little drunk myself.

"I love you very much, my darling," Sandra began dictating in Spanish. "I think of you every day…"

"Not so fast!" I was having trouble keeping up.

Moments later—I don't know how it happened—we were rolling together on the bed.

"*Ay, papacito.* Give it to me! *Llenamelo de leche!* Fuck me full of cream!"

The second it was over she resumed the dictation:

"I think of you every day…"

We finished off the tequila, and then she put on a baggy Wisconsin sweatshirt, a gift from some college boy, and began singing, "*On Wisconsin, on Wisconsin, grand old badger state!*"

"That's good! That's very good!"

"What does it mean, badger?"

"A badger is like a woodchuck. You know woodchuck?"

"No."

"It's like a wolverine, actually. You know wolverine?"

"No."

"A wolverine is sort of a combination of a woodchuck and a weasel. And a skunk. You know weasel?"

"No."

"A weasel is like a ferret…"

3

BANDITS HELD UP PROFUNDA'S TAXI, on Insurgentes, near Colonia San Felipe del Real. I went to the Navy Rose in the afternoon. It was the day of Paulo's birthday party. Angel Mike was behind the bar. He told me Profunda wanted to see me in her room. I found her crying. There was blood on her sweater, and one eye was swollen almost shut.

"*Por qué?*" she sobbed. "*Por qué, mi vida?* Why? Why?"

I tried to talk to her but it was useless. She was hysterical. I went back to the bar and got a bottle of tequila, two glasses, some quartered limes and a saltshaker on a lacquered tin tray. All on credit, of course. I wasn't exactly bucks up.

We sat close together on the soiled bed and had a drink, then another. I put my arm around Profunda. I patted her and hugged her, I smooched it up with her. I licked Profunda's wet face like a puppy. Black rivers of mascara ran from her weeping eyes, draining into my mouth. Her left cheek was swollen and blackened; her ear was crusted with dried blood. I unbuttoned her sweater and took out her mammoth breasts and kissed them, then I slipped my hand under her skirt and fingered her pussy while we got drunk, in order to take her mind off her troubles.

"*Ay, papacito,*" she murmured, stuffing a swollen nipple into my mouth. "*No te vayas, papacito. Me gustas mucho. Oof! Yo te quiero, corazón. Te quiero mucho a ti!*"

She sagged against me, sobbing and moaning, breathing deeply as my fingers swirled like tentacles inside her slippery cunt. She was sopping wet. My prescription was working. She was coming around. Booze and lust are an excellent remedy for grief.

Profunda was heartbroken. Her goodness was her undoing. She was sentimental. She placed her fellow human beings too high in her heart. She thought people were better than they were. It wasn't the money. She was crying for *them*. I had to agree. They were rotten, those bastards, stealing from their own kind. They took her purse, and then they felt her up and called her a whore. I didn't know how to comfort her, except by getting her drunk and letting her pour it out. I felt lousy, humiliated; it was as if *I* had robbed her. I felt that *I* was the criminal, that *I* had betrayed her.

After Profunda came I wiped my hand off on her skirt, then I gave her tits a final squeeze and stuffed them back inside her sweater.

"*Ay, mi madre,*" she whispered, breathing in my face. "*No te vayas, corazón.* Do not leave me."

"I'm not going," I said in Spanish. "*We're* going. We're going together, to Paulo's birthday party. *Vámanos!*'

Paulo's room was a block from the Navy Rose. It was filled with cooking smells. The paint on the walls was cracked and cockroaches scurried everywhere. Paper streamers and balloons adorned the dismal cell. A toy-like phonograph whirled a stack of records. Javier Solis wailed "*Sombras Nada Mas,*" and Amalia Mendoza belted out "*Vas Conmigo.*" Strong stuff, raw emotion. A dozen people were milling around, gabbing and drinking. Reymundo arrived with another pouf, a real street Arab very much like himself. And Glorieta, in a pink-blonde wig and a smashing red taffeta dress. Glorieta was also a *peinadora*. He worked at Reymundo's *salon de belleza*. Cookies and Magdelena popped in, two whores from the Navy Rose. Cookies was an iceberg as usual, a perfect plastic doll, but Magda smiled and made small talk with me. I'd written several letters for her to a cattle baron from San Antonio. Angel Mike, the bartender, appeared briefly, but he seemed uneasy, and when Reymundo asked him to dance, his face fell and he left abruptly.

I danced with Profunda. She was surprisingly light and nimble on her feet, while her round ponderous body rocked to and fro like an enormous turtle made out of jello. Her titties jiggled with excitement. She was almost squirting in her pants. This was the moment to hand her over to somebody. I looked around. It was all queers and lesbians except for Profunda and myself. Then I spotted a hunchback who was an emcee at a *turista* joint on Avenida Juárez. He announced the strippers. I'd seen him on stage. He was dancing with one of the lesbians, smiling at everybody, servile as a puppy. At my insistence, Profunda danced with him, with the hunchback. I thought she might go for him; he was tall for a hunchback and not bad looking, but nothing doing. While they danced she kept making goo-goo eyes at me over his hump.

Then came a knock on the door. It was the flunky from the bakery with the cake in his arms. He brought it in flaming, blazing with dancing candles. It was a magic moment. The stooge put the cake down on the table and Paulo leaned over and blew out the candles. It took him two puffs. There were a lot of candles.

Then things went off on a bum tangent. Reymundo and Glorieta converged on the bakery stooge. They were looped and spoiling for a little malicious horseplay. Jabbering like monkeys they seized the bewildered man and buffeted him around like a ping-pong ball. They scooped some white frosting off the cake and smeared it on his face, transforming him into a clown. They stepped back and surveyed their work, and Glorieta shoved a banana in his mouth. After a chorus of shrill laughter they shouted orders at him in broken English; they pushed him and tripped him, they pelted him with ice cubes. The man was somewhat dull-witted; he was confused and almost in tears. I stepped in and called a halt to it. After issuing a few verbal threats I gave the man a five-dollar bill and sent him on his way. Reymundo and Glorieta withdrew sullenly. They were miffed, but no more than that, and a moment later the incident was forgotten. We all devoured slices of sponge cake and pistachio ice cream graciously served by Paulo himself, the birthday boy.

"*Bailamos?*" Paulo asked me after wiping his face with a napkin. "Would you like to dance?"

"*Como no?*" I said, grasping his frail shoulders. Paulo was drunk and so was I. I shook his hand and wished him a happy birthday. Then we danced to "Mambo Italiano." Paulo led, and I was thankful for that. Paulo was a terrific dancer.

Around four a.m. I wobbled back to the Navy Rose, burst through the swinging doors and stood reeling at the edge of the deserted dance floor. Five or six of the girls were sleeping in the booths pulled close to the glowing *calientón,* clustered like little pigs around a sow's belly. Angel Mike was snoring with his head on the bar. The faintly pulsing jukebox whirled its spectral colors over the walls. At a table in the rear near the toilet a young soldier was asleep in his vomit.

The Navy Rose, a haven for sleepers. Everyone was snoring away like mad. *Ho hum!* I found Profunda's booth and give her a good jolt with my elbow and obligingly she squirmed over to make a place for me.

I'm lying now with my head in Profunda's lap. She is awake. I'm laughing as I drift off to sleep looking up at Profunda's eyes that glisten like moist grubs. *Even her eyes are fat!* Profunda speaks to me tenderly: "*My leetle chiquitito... Pobrecito! Andas borracho corazón.* You are too dronk, understand? *Ho hum! Tienes hambre, corazón?* What is it? *Eh?* Are you sad? *Ah!* Why do you laugh? *Malcriado! En qué piensas?* Why do you not speak to me? *Mira, mi vida,* this is not the way of a husband. Sweetheart, lessgo my house. You are going to call a taxi, understand? *Psst, Miguel, qué horas son? Las cuatro? Válgame Diós!* Four o'clock in the morning and look at us. Soon it will be five o'clock and then six and then seven. *Ay mi madre,* the *bebés* will be hungry. *Comen mucho los niños. Mi vida,* wake up, *mi vida.* You weel buy pants for my *bebés.* I gotta three *bebés;* he only gotta one pair of pants. *Casate conmigo, corazón.* You are a good man. I believe it. *Ah?* What is the matter with you? *Ay, mi madre,* you are asleep. Sleep well, *pobrecito. Duermete feliz, my leetle chiquitito..."*

4

"I'VE FOUND A CITY," Roscoe informed me one night as we were standing at the bar at the Rosita Club hooking down ten-cent tequilas. It was a regular thing with Roscoe, this business of finding a city. It was a phase. When it came over him, this finding-a-city mood, he'd spend hours in the public library studying the maps in the world, searching for the ideal city where, as he never failed to assure me, he would be content to spend the rest of his life.

Always it started out more or less as a joke. Or at least Roscoe was half joking...at first. Then he'd begin to believe in the dream. That he was actually going there, I mean. He'd conjure up so much enthusiasm that I too would begin to believe that he was really going through with it this time. Once some degree of credibility was established relative to the venture the conversation would switch to the nuts and bolts of exactly how he'd pull it off, the great escape. The procedure would be, theoretically—and the word 'theoretically' is important here—to get a job, save a bundle, buy survival equipment, get a passport, pack a suitcase, and, most important, *buy a ticket and get on the plane or the train or wherever.* But for Roscoe, somewhere along the way, the process always broke down. He'd go into it enthusiastically enough—at first. But always a certain distance and no further. Roscoe's downfall was that he couldn't help wondering what was around the next corner, I mean immediately. That was the essence of his personality and his most positive quality. With Roscoe it was always one more drink, one more look at the stars, one more wobble around the block before turning in, because who knows what might happen? Roscoe's immediate involvement with life tended to preclude any long-range plans.

"Let's hit for Copenhagen." How many times had I heard Roscoe say that? Or Rome. Or Madrid. Or Paris. Or Amsterdam, Venice, Florence, Istanbul, Hong Kong, Katmandu, or even New York. Usually if the city was in the United States, it was at least on the opposite coast. As long as it was *somewhere else*... Someplace far away, where, miraculously, everything would be different. Many times, to give Roscoe credit, he actually left, but he'd start out for the Big Apple and wind up in Chagrin Falls, Ohio. That was the story of his life.

Once Roscoe was mentally hooked on a city he'd read everything he could find about the city and he'd talk constantly about the city. The city, the city, became his whole world: the miraculous far-off city that contained the prescribed remedy for everything that was wrong with him. He dreamed the city, he lived the city; he saturated his consciousness with it. If the city was Copenhagen, for example, then it was Copenhagen, twenty-four hours a day. He ate Copenhagen, he drank Copenhagen, he pissed Copenhagen. This was Roscoe's way, conscious or unconscious, of attempting to galvanize himself into *action*. He was trying desperately to overcome his lethal inertia. Once he was caught up in the idea of the city—and it was always that, with Roscoe, not the city itself, but the *idea* of the city—a startling change would come over him. Suddenly Roscoe had a Purpose. His energies polarized—for as long as the spell lasted.

This time Roscoe's chosen city was Machu Picchu, the lost fortress-city of the Incas perched high in the Peruvian Andes, two thousand feet above the Urubamba River. Probably his choice had something to do with Minga, the Peruvian Pelvis, his squeeze from the Luz de Luna. Since his fling with her any mention of Peru sent him into raptures.

"It's a city in the clouds," he chirped euphorically. "Everything is made out of stone. No lawns to mow or any of that. They chew coca leaves all day long. The priests come around to the doorways ringing little bells. They eat yak butter and bake their own bread. Sound like a pretty good life?"

Later, we repaired to the Palmeras Club on *Mariscal* south of *Calle Ugarte*. The Palmeras Club wasn't much from the outside, a green-lettered sign jutting out high over the street, topped with a pink neon palm tree. A dull red building with a chipped cracked facade and a gas meter dangling off the wall, and brown swinging doors with brass kick plates.

Inside there was a long bar hooked at the end like a question mark. The walls of the Palmeras Club were splashed with Rousseau-like frescoes, as if *Le Douanier* had stopped in for a few drinks and brought along his brushes. A waxed dance floor and an ancient jukebox were the main features of a large room divided down the center by a double row of booths jammed back to back where the girls congregated, played cards, gossiped and slept. On the other side of the booths a roomy sector opened onto the dance floor, and beyond that customers sat at tables, or mushed it up with girls in booths along the far wall. Upstairs, a balcony-like affair was open on special nights, such as Cinco de Mayo or soldiers' payday night. Couples, whores and their clients, would sit at small round tables peering over the railing at the dancers swirling below while waiters bounded up the stairs three steps at a time with trays of drinks. From time to time Indian beggar women wrapped in serapes would traipse in and out, as well as street vendors with stacks of sombreros and open cases crammed with watches, rings, sunglasses and other glittery junk. Spiffy photographers darted here and there, and sometimes very young girls carrying steaming pails of tamales covered with white napkins would peer cautiously in the door.

A reeking urinal perfectly open to everything squatted at the rear of the dance floor. You'd pause in the middle of a Mexican polka and stand holding your girl's hand while you pissed in the dented tin trough along with half a dozen tough-looking hombres.

An incident I witnessed once at the Palmeras Club could almost have been a scene from a Greek drama—or a comedy. It was afternoon. Things were slow. A whore pinned a donkey tail, an actual one, on the ass of an old man's trousers. The old man had been drinking in the Palmeras Club all day. He was apparently on a last fling, laughingly goosing the girls, practically in his second childhood. He was very rugged, with a crinkled face, possibly a seafaring man. After they'd pinned the donkey's tail to his pants, the girls laughed and jibed at him for an hour or more while he obligingly pranced around the dance floor like a drunken satyr before he discovered that he'd literally been a made an ass of. But he took it all in good graces and, like a good old salt, which I'm sure he was, even bought a round of drinks for everyone.

The girls' rooms, the *cuartos*, at the Palmeras Club were out in back. They were outdoor cribs, actually, encircling a small courtyard. You walked past the urinal, through a door, down a narrow, crooked hallway, through another door, and there it was, the courtyard. The rooms themselves were plaster of Paris caves lubricated with a greenish phosphorescence. Here the girls, when they weren't fucking, would snooze or apply their mascara behind scarred wooden doors. In each room it was the same. The musty bunk with its smooth brown sheets, the sputtering saint's candle, the cracked mirror taped to the wall, the trampled dirt floor, the ceramic water jug, the dented tin basin for washing the pricks of the customers, and piles of dirty clothes and cats' nests and orange rinds and other garbage under the bed.

After the tussle was over you'd stroll out into the courtyard, which was littered with straw and partially paved with stones. A section of galvanized pipe spouted a jet of clear water that pierced a blue-green slime of algae floating on the surface of a wooden drinking trough. Pigs, dogs, cats and kittens cavorted, and a goat, tethered to a stake in the middle of the yard, brayed idiotically. And every once in a while one of the scarred wooden doors in the encircling ring of cribs would open and a basin of water was emptied—*sploosh*—on the paving stones. I don't know why, but here the world seemed to me to be beautifully intact—a sordid world, yet somehow fresh and curiously innocent—and if angels should descend from heaven tonight and order every human soldier to fix bayonets and stand, I'd pick as my little patch of ground to stand on and defend, this bleak mud and stone courtyard behind the Palmeras Club.

Tonight, there was an oyster cart stationed at the end of the bar near the door, a white wooden wagon on rubber wheels filled with chipped ice and chilled oysters, and a fat guy in a white apron was shucking oysters and slopping on sauce and handing them out as fast as he could. A bonanza night, with everyone eating, drinking, gabbling.

Standing at the bar, drunk as a seahorse, I half listened to Roscoe as he slurped down oyster after oyster, his bloodshot eyes rimmed with white circles of frog spit. Impaled on the impossible pinnacles of his shipwrecked life, he was raving. Peru…the lost city of the Incas perched high above the dizzying green gorge of the Urubamba. Peru, the volcanoes on the march, the dreamy, creamy clouds. Peru! So help me God, it was starting to get a grip on me, too. Peru, the masturbator's paradise! Peru, the jacked-off essence of everything that's Indian and feminine and fierce and eternal. It was beautiful, the fatalism of it. It was like falling into the center of a flower, like drowning in a pool of nectar.

"I had a dream last night," Roscoe said. "About Charleston. I was coming home from the Civil War. They were leading me into the city. The light blinded my eyes. I must have been wounded. The mansions on Church Street, the white columns, so white, and the green trees and the green, green lawns and the birdbaths... Cottonwood blossoms were falling softly, white like snowflakes. Do they have cottonwoods in Charleston? I can't remember. You must have passed through there. But it doesn't matter. Anything is possible in a dream. It was beautiful. I was coming home from the war. 'Is this Charleston?' I kept asking. 'Is this Charleston?' And when I woke up, I was crying...

"Yeah...I keep going to the library and looking at all the maps in the atlases. Just pissing the time away and dreaming about things, about places I'd like to be. Besides here, I mean. Cities! Cities like London, Paris, Madrid... LA, even—anyplace but here! Even little towns, places like Twin Falls, Idaho, or Duluth, Minnesota. Or Grand Junction, Colorado. I never liked Colorado much for some reason. But I like Wyoming. Especially Casper, Wyoming. I had a part-time job there once, sweeping up in a drugstore, four hours a week..."

We ate more oysters, *osteones*. The Halcones strolled in, a mariachi band with whom Roscoe and I were on drinking terms. The leader, Juvencio, bought us a round and then they strolled out. The girls were padding around in transparent shifts or ballet-tight mini-costumes. A marimba band was setting up in the front near the oyster cart, and it made a beautiful picture, the flashy hawk-nosed guy with his vibes in his white sport coat while behind him the fat sweating genie was shucking oysters.

I was feeling jolly, so I ordered up a bottle of Urdiñola, Roscoe's favorite poison, and two glasses.

"But do you know, brother, what I really regret?" Roscoe continued. "That time in Miami when I was going to take the boat to Bimini but I got drunk and passed out in the men's room of the Mermaid Lounge on Northeast 51st Street. And I fucking missed the boat. That's the only thing in my life I really regret. Believe this, Jerz: I could have been *happy* in Bimini..."

The "Real Mexico" was also a favorite theme. Roscoe's "Real Mexico" was Zihuatenejo, deep in "Mexican Polynesia," near the island of Ixtapa, where a wide jungle river meets the sea—so Roscoe maintained—between two graceful palms. There was a sunken wreck offshore, a Spanish galleon, he insisted, and the bay, protected by rugged mountains, was alive with sharks. He was fascinated by the lean-tos of the shark hunters and turtle fishermen that he'd once seen on the shores of Magdalena Bay.

"What a way to *live*," he'd insist. "You've got your skiff and your hooks and your tackle, your gun and your machete and your bedroll. You fucking build yourself a lean-to on the beach..."

Roscoe could go on for hours about the thatched-roof village, the shark livers strung up to dry in the sun, and the palm trees—two of them, poised at the edge of the sea, on either side of the wide river. And bare-breasted women were washing their clothes in the river, and young girls were rinsing their long black hair. The Real Mexico. It was a beautiful dream, and I have to admit that I bought into it, at least to some extent.

So much for the dream: let's get down to the reality of it. Roscoe and I arrived in El Paso in a boxcar. We climbed up from the tracks on South El Paso Street and popped into the ultra-homey Hollywood Café, where, grimy as we were, we immediately got a line on jobs as greens keepers at the Lone Star Golf Course. We found cheap digs at the

Paradise Motel, and as soon as payday rolled around we began hitting the cantinas across the river on Mariscal Street. Then Roscoe met Pilar and decided to get serious about life. He married her, brought her to the US, got a 'real' job at Sears, and they moved into an apartment on Prospect.

I stayed on at the Paradise Motel and got myself a gig driving a pie delivery truck. It was beautiful. My whole day was pies, pies, pies. Apple, pecan, banana cream, sweet potato, lemon meringue. *Pies!* I don't know why pies should be hilarious in themselves, but they are. Maybe it's the association with the old-time slapstick movies. I was perpetually in a good mood. It felt like I was breathing laughing gas. The boss said I was handing out too many samples and threatened to fire me, but it was actually good business, giving the customers a taste like that, getting them hooked...

Roscoe and I went back to the Hollywood Café again and again. It was *chorizo* heaven, the cheapest breakfast in town, and somehow the Hollywood Café has remained in my mind as a landmark, a symbol of that first golden Juárez period. It was a period rich in encounters, events, mysteries, mating, food, drink and talk.

.

5

ON THE NIGHT BEFORE THANKSGIVING there was an enormous round moon in the sky, a golden moon filled with *Urdiñola*, and in Colonia Alta Vista this golden *Urdiñola* moon was balanced at the end of the narrow dirt street with clusters of tiny mud huts choking it in on either side, an effect so magical it was as if madness itself had descended on Ciudad Juárez. Nearly a year had passed since that first day at the Hollywood Café. Roscoe had been fired from the Sears job for dipping into the till. He'd lost the apartment on Prospect, too, and he and Pilar had moved in with the in-laws on *Calle* O in Colonia Alta Vista. I still had the pie delivery job—one of my longest runs on any job—and my room at the Paradise Motel, but if Roscoe and I had been drinking all night on Mariscal Street I'd sometimes stay over in Colonia Alta Vista, much to Pilar's disgust.

Present at the Thanksgiving feast were Monalisa and Salvador, Pilar's mother and father, and Felisa, the elder sister, who worked at the Navy Rose, Felisa's daughter, Lucinda who was ten, Roscoe and myself; also Javier, "Tony," an infant. Tony's mother, Josefina, the eldest sister, formerly a *mesera* at the Gusano Club, was soon to arrive. She'd been whoring in Matamoros and had made the long trip by bus and was now en route to Colonia Alta Vista in a taxi with the turkey and trimmings and number two sister Felisa's six-month old half-American daughter Guadalupe, "Bebé Linda."

The day before, as dusk was falling and the gigantic *Urdiñola* moon was just beginning to peer over the horizon, I watched Monalisa and Felisa's little Lucinda stroll to the polluted creek that flows through the Colonia Alta Vista and stand gazing at the dirty water. Lucinda was clutching a grimy, naked, one-legged doll.

"Stay close to me," Monalisa cautioned. "*El Cucuy* will get you!"

"No! No!" Lucinda was so frightened she almost dropped her doll in the canal. In Mexico, children and even adults believe in *El Cucuy*, a humpbacked boogeyman with glowing red eyes. When Monalisa noticed that Lucinda had been properly intimidated, she smiled confidently to herself, and they walked back to the hut, holding hands.

Felisa was by far the most passionate of the daughters, and certainly the most fetching, or so I thought, but this was before I laid eyes on Ysela, the youngest daughter, the occasional mistress of boxer Juan "El Indio" Mendoza. But more about Ysela later...

"*Mucho corazón*" is what they said about Felisa on Mariscal Street. But they said it in the sense of "too much heart". Meaning she was too passionate, too good, too generous, too alive. Felisa drank hard and she fell in love hard and often. She burned with a bright interior flame that was quickly consuming her. Like all the girls in the family, and practically all the girls in Colonia Alta Vista, she'd been whoring since her early teens. But Felisa wasn't cut out for a whore, not in my estimation. There was nothing mercenary in her nature, nothing of "the little shopkeeper", which must be present in the soul of the successful whore. She had too much heart, which is a left-handed way of saying that if you're feeble-minded and half dead, you'll get through life without any trouble. Felisa gave too easily, too much and too often. When she gave, she gave everything, immediately, desperately, and she expected, and almost never received, the same from others.

Sometimes when I stayed over I'd wake up when Felisa came home in a taxi at dawn, and I'd watch her as she sat on a milk crate in the greenish half-light of the saint's candle fixing her face in a splinter of broken mirror taped to the wall and belting down bolts of courage from a pint of tequila she took from her purse. The taxi would wait, the driver snoring at the wheel for twenty minutes or an hour. Then she'd be off again. Sometimes she was gone for days, and frequently she was absent from work at the Navy Rose Club.

Roscoe had brought his newspaper with him to the festivities, neatly folded, tucked under his arm as always. That newspaper was a badge. It was his passport, his *carte d'identité*. It meant that Roscoe Longworth still belonged to the human race.

Earlier Roscoe and I had walked to the tiny grocery store near the Papagayo Cantina which called itself simply "*Abarrotes*", and brought back two bottles of Urdiñola, "*Licor de Caballeros*." This was our contribution to the feast.

I cracked open one of the bottles and poured out a drop for everybody, then handed the nearly full bottle to Salvador, Pilar's father, who took me gently by the arm. We ducked under the low door of the adobe hut and walked outside into the dirt yard. There he talked to me at considerable length, and with great warmth and enthusiasm, frequently bursting into tears or laughter and tears and then laughter again, slapping his thigh.

The entire speech, his personal history, the story of his life, more or less, went on for better than an hour while we waited for Josefina, the Whore of Matamoros, to arrive with the food. As I watched Salvador doing his funny little dance on one foot, hopping and slapping the dust out of his thigh, I found myself actually witnessing scenes from his life. I was with him, tramping through the dust, places I'd never been, seeing the world through his eyes, swinging a grub hoe, scooping up the fresh earth of plowed fields in my two hands. I smelled the warm hides of animals, the musk of strange women. With me always, like a presence, was the mingled aroma of sweat and tobacco and dust— *my* smell. I was a beast of burden stumbling forward in darkness, a brute bellowing under the hammer. I was the man himself, his sweat, his stink, his dreary hours of toil, his longing for sleep, his dumb hope.

Salvador was a beast of burden and yet there was something of the *brujo* about the man. He had the face of an ancient clown, a comical mug that was seamed and creased like an old catcher's mitt. This man had been over the road and still there was something in him that hadn't given up. He opened himself to me as though I were an old and understanding friend, a friend he had known all his life.

Monalisa, Pilar's mother, would sit for hours by the *calientón*, sewing. The most singular facet of Monalisa's character was her extraordinary composure. She had a moth-eaten brown tweed coat that she wore at all times, even to sleep. In the afternoons she'd drag one of the wooden milk crates outside and sit in the sun, her serene high-boned face glowing, her little sewing things on her lap.

Just as Salvador and I were killing off the fifth of Urdiñola in the yard, the headlights of a taxi came bobbling up the road, fizzing acid-orange on the pulverized dust at our feet. Which meant that Josefina had arrived at last with the grub. I watched her ducking through the door with the turkey under her arm and dragging Bebé Linda by the hand. A big devil...well-rounded, obviously healthy, not at all bad to look at...but her *seriousness* appalled me. Moments later Pilar grudgingly introduced us in her supercilious, overly formal way: "I would like to present to you my sister, Josefina..." She might as well have said she was Jo-Jo the Dogfaced Boy for all I cared. For the life of me I couldn't picture this woman holding court in a cantina, a whorehouse, mind you, getting a man all lathered up and dragging him off to her room. She'd met an American—so we learned—a truck driver, a *trocero*, and now he was keeping her, had given her money and paid her bus fare. And more was forthcoming, she proudly announced to Pilar and Felisa.

Josefina had brought the eats for the feast in the taxi, making Roscoe feel small (so she thought, but she didn't know him yet) as the ineffectual head of the household, newly married, jobless, broke, and camping in Colonia Alta Vista with his in-laws and even having the audacity to bring along his penniless writer pal—me. Right from the beginning, Josefina was extremely scornful of Roscoe and me. She pegged us for a couple of idlers, and of course she was right. All the same, her haughty manner made me laugh. You'd have thought she'd been spending a fortnight at Buckingham Palace instead of selling her ass down in Matamoros.

Thanksgiving dinner in Colonia Alta Vista also marked the beginning of Pilar's turning against me. It was as if Josefina's arrival had helped her to see me in a truer light. She realized that I wasn't serious about life and that I was definitely a bad influence on Roscoe...

But the dinner! The table was sagging under the weight of the food. I'm not exaggerating. It was a dazzling spread. A gigantic turkey, glazed, steaming hot from the bakery oven, with plenty of dressing, rice and beans, *mole de ajo*, cranberry sauce, smoking stacks of corn tortillas, tamales, and hot crusty bread fresh from the *panaderia* on 16 *de Septiembre* Street. We pounced rabidly on the food, and afterwards, of course, there were *dulces* and *café* for everyone.

Roscoe and I sat on the two red plastic chairs. The others sat on wooden milk crates. The light from a kerosene lantern threw our huge flickering shadows on the leprous walls and cast an eerie, smoky glow over the rickety table around which we huddled like a family of potato-eaters. In addition to the Urdiñola there was wine, *Vino Tinto de Misión de Santo Tomas*, which Roscoe and Salvador and I drank unrelentingly throughout the meal, much to the disgust of the women, except for Monalisa who remained as always "above the storm".

Midway through the dinner, Cesar Wong, Felisa's half-Chinese suitor, came to take her out to a movie. Characteristically, Cesar Wong declined to sit down at the table with us. After much bowing and scraping, he hovered meekly into a corner while we stuffed ourselves like pigs. Cesar Wong was delicately handsome, self-effacing, excessively polite, extremely serious, clean to a fault and neat—even poison neat. He was an apprentice tailor, attended church regularly and owned a car. I found his excessive humility embarrassing. Cesar Wong worshipped Felisa but she treated him like dirt. Felisa had a standing offer of marriage from Cesar Wong. Not only that, but he'd repeatedly begged her to allow him to support her, in a private apartment, with no strings attached, in order to help her break away from the life on Mariscal Street. But Felisa didn't want to break away from the life on Mariscal Street, because that was her life. Cesar Wong was a jerk, a sucker, a victim, but Cesar Wong was also something else: Cesar Wong was a hero of love—just as Felisa, in her own way, was a hero of love. Cesar Wong would gladly have licked the shit off Felisa's boots if she'd let him, but Felisa preferred to leave him standing in the vestibule with his hat in his hand while an army of men marched between her legs.

When the time came for the *café* and the *dulces*, the women huddled together, chattering and speculating about Josefina's cowboy, how much he made, etc. Already they were calibrating his paycheck in terms of stoves, refrigerators, pots, pans, beans and tortillas, blankets and baby shoes.

Later, after I was standing outside, talking with Salvador and Roscoe, another taxi arrived. This time it was Ysela, the youngest sister, the boxer's mistress, with a child's white dress. Monalisa and little Lucinda came out to greet her and Ysela held up the dress for Lucinda to see.

"Look, *mihija*," Monalisa murmured. "How beautiful. For your Confirmation."

"Oh, I love it," Lucinda exclaimed delightedly. "Thank you, Aunt Ysela, thank you so much! Can I try it on?"

Monalisa and Lucinda went back into the hut. Ysela walked to a nearby hut. I followed, entranced. The door of the hut was open. Ysela went inside. I stepped to the door, pulled aside a dusty burlap curtain and saw a makeshift altar illuminated by many glowing candles. Ysela was kneeling before an effigy of the Virgin de la Soledad that closely resembled the original I'd once seen in the Templo de la Soledad in Oaxaca: an embroidered black gown, a golden crown and a somewhat grim expression, as if she were admonishing the petitioner: "You made your bed, now lie in it."

Ysela stood up, crossed herself and made for the door. I held the curtain open for her.

"*Soy muy puta, pero soy muy Católica,*" she blurted, scarcely looking at me. "I'm a whore, yes, but I'm a Catholic," is what I took her words to mean. Ysela was a beautiful woman. There was something of the *bruja* about her, something of the sorceress, a dark mysterious sexuality that reflected both her sister Felisa's tragic quality and her own special brand of blind courageous defiance. I stood in the doorway of the makeshift temple and watched her march back to her taxi and speed away.

Right after Christmas I lost my pie delivery job for letting too many customers taste my wares, Simple Simon that I was, and I began camping three and four nights a week with Roscoe and the family in Colonia Alta Vista. This was our daily life: we sat around the *calientón*, blue with cold, roasting *pepitas,* pumpkin seeds, on a flattened piece of tin and munching them all day long like a troupe of feeble-minded chimpanzees. *Platicando,* as they say. Talking! When I look back on it, the inane conversations, the idiotic topics we discussed, I think, and I often thought at the time, that the only difference between Monalisa's hut in Colonia Alta Vista and a lunatic asylum is that in Colonia Alta Vista there were no bars on the windows.

A favorite topic: What was it like *en el otro lado,* on the other side of the river? They, the women and children, confidently imagined that El Paso was a paradise, a magical city flowing with milk and honey. To have told them the truth would have been cruel and monstrous. To be honest, it never even crossed my mind. I saw no reason to dent their fantasy since I figured they would never make it across the border anyway. Instead, I told them glowing lies about America, whatever I thought they wanted to hear.

Perpetually in view, as we chattered away, were the white towers of El Paso, most prominently the El Cortez Hotel and the two monolithic bank buildings. It was like seeing Istanbul from the poppy fields. We were nomads camped on the edge of the American Desert, refugees perched on the outskirts of a glittering mirage that called itself America. We were packrats, rodents, ground squirrels. We were a host of prairie dogs, a hive of conies, a city of gophers poking our furry heads out of dusty holes in the earth.

In late afternoon, as the slanting rays of the sun that had baked the plaster of Paris saints drying on the rooftops of the shantytown began to bounce off the glittering towers of El Paso across the river, a fleet of battered yellow taxis would arrive, taxi after taxi, stirring up a furious cloud of dust, and young girls, some in their early teens, would emerge from the hovels, decked out in evening gowns and low-cut dresses. They were on their way to work in the cantinas on Mariscal Street. In a very few years, this would be little Lucinda's fate: in order to put food on the table, she would have to open her legs for the Americans.

One morning I met Victor and Gustavo, Pilar's cousins, both in their early twenties. We were standing in front of Monalisa's hut. It was a bright, sunny day. The wind blew a tumbleweed past us, and suddenly the air was filled with dust. Behind the shantytown the El Paso cityscape loomed like a shimmering mirage.

"They hunted us like rabbits," Victor said. "We ran but we couldn't get away. There was too many of them. They killed my father and my brother."

"They told us *manos arriba! Manos arriba!*" Gustavo added. "We put our hands up, but they started shooting. What can we do? We can't do nothing."

I couldn't figure out what they were talking about until Monalisa emerged from the hut and showed me a page from the newspaper *El Diario,* a photo of two slain men, and the headline, *"Los Vigilantes mataron a dos migrantes."* "Border Vigilantes kill two immigrants."

Victor, tearful, pointed at one of the men in the photo. "That's our father."

Monalisa folded the newspaper and sat down on her milk crate with her little sewing things in her lap, perfectly serene and composed as always, her gaze fixed on the El Paso towers, gleaming in the morning sun.

"There will be no place in heaven for those who have treated the poor so shamefully," she murmured.

During this period of extreme poverty I made scavenging expeditions to El Paso. I walked boldly into restaurants, grabbed discarded plates, gobbled the leavings and left. I lived by scrounging, a predatory existence but an exhilarating one, walking a good twenty miles a day, my heart pumping, my blood circulating, and my senses alive. Recently I saw in a film a pack of wild African hunting dogs on a run, loping at a steady pace across the veldt, with every nose tuned to the scent, and I thought immediately of my El Paso-Juárez life. It wasn't a bad life.

It was a good life. I simply reverted to an earlier, food-gatherer stage of evolution. Once this was accomplished, I felt my being come sharply into focus. I suddenly felt: *here I am*, again and still, roving over the land in search of food. If the world was crazy, if it was all a dream, at least this one thing was certain and real. It's amazing how simple life becomes when you forget about going through channels. Instead of getting a job in order to get money in order to get food, why not simply get food?

I lived the life of a primitive hunter, a food-gatherer. The hunt was my time to be alone with my soul, and the constant walking stimulated both mental activity and digestion. It was stimulating in every way. When you're hungry, you're on the alert; and when you're on the alert, all sorts of things happen. I was thrilled to realize that, while as a human being I might be a failure, as an animal I was quite self-sufficient, quite healthy, quite omnivorous. It gave me a new respect for myself. It made me aware of a physical buoyancy, a certain stone-age wisdom that was inseparable from my being. Deep down in the nexus of instinctive fibers was an entity that took life in stride. I discovered, to my surprise and delight, that I was wearing a gorilla suit underneath my shirt.

The gorilla was really quite an amiable fellow. The gorilla was happy. He could munch green leaves and tender bamboo shoots, and he could fart and he could grunt and smack his lips. That was enough. The gorilla had a soul—a soul big enough to fit inside his chest. When the gorilla had filled his stomach, he would lie on his back and play with his toes and gaze joyfully up at the sky. When he fell asleep, his soul flew out of his mouth and wandered happily over the earth, and when he woke up, at the instant of awakening, his soul flew back into his mouth and perched once again inside his chest, ready for another day.

At night it was immensely still in Colonia Alta Vista. There was no electricity, hence no radios or televisions. In

the hut it was silent except for the friendly *bong* of the
calientón and the scraping of the wind, always the wind,
scouring and eroding away. And the sudden scampering of
cat feet across the tin roof... A bedraggled orange cat
came around. Needless to say we never fed it. That orange
cat passed its time hunting lizards or sitting patiently on its
paws in front of the gopher holes that pocked the dirt
plain that sloped away from Monalisa's hut down to the
putrid canal where marijuana grew wild. She, the cat, left
half-chewed lizards with gaping mouths and savage
glittering eyes in front of the door. The severed tails
whipped furiously in the dust.

One night, just a few hovels away, a man went berserk
after downing a bottle of tequila and hacked his infant
daughter to pieces with a machete. We saw the *federales*
arrive, and the ambulance when it came in the morning,
and the blood on the walls. The incident made the front
page of *La Alarma*, the sensational tabloid newspaper.

Another thing I remember: scorpions. There were a lot
of them in Colonia Alta Vista. For some reason scorpions
like the company of humans; they prefer to be indoors.
Frequently you'd hear a sudden cry ring out, in the middle
of the night, "*Alacrán!*" And everybody scatters, clutching
blankets and pillows. In other words, pandemonium. Or
Roscoe and I would come in drunk from Mariscal Street,
and Roscoe would shout, "*Alacrán!*" And everybody
sleeping on the bed and on the floor would leap up, half
nuts with paranoia, and Roscoe, with me right behind him,
would make a dive for a choice sleeping spot.

In the mornings I'd awaken to the sound of the
Menudo Man calling, "*MEN-udo! MEN-udo!*" He walked
all through the hills like a donkey, balancing his heavy
kettle of steaming *menudo* on a smooth wooden pole slung
across his shoulders. I'd go to the door with a bowl; he'd
dip out the *menudo* with a ladle. He'd hover there with one
arm hooked over his pole, working the ladle, his breath
standing in the air, his bristled face chapped raw and his

shrewd little eyes dancing under a tattered hat brim. I never knew exactly how much the stuff cost. I'd give him pennies, *centavos*, quarters, nickels. If there were too few coins he'd look at me sternly. I'd drop a few more *centavos* into his palm and he'd go away, apparently satisfied.

I'd sit down at the table with my bowl of *menudo* and cut an onion in half. Outside, roosters were crowing and the Menudo Man was shouting down the alley, "*MEN-udo! MEN-udo!*" How simple life seemed in those moments.

About then the lumbering water truck would come grinding up the rutted dirt road with its hose like an elephant's trunk tied up in back. Women emerge from the huts with basins, bottles and jars, and men step out of their doorways, stretching and yawning like idiots. An old woman stands in the middle of the street pissing like a cow, legs apart, her skirts hitched up around her knees. Lizards skitter, chickens and goats cavort everywhere, rags flap on the clotheslines. The sun shines brightly on the plaster of Paris statuettes—the Virgin of Guadalupe, the Madonna and Child, Jesus baring His sacred heart—drying on the rooftops.

In the mornings in Mexico everything is *limpiado*, washed clean by the shining, brimming light. The night in Mexico is full of danger. There are bandits, demons, cults and assassins. You feel this. In the morning, the world is round and shining. The sunlight splashes on the dust, on your feet. The sand glitters in the bricks. The morning brings relief and joy, a reason to say, *thank you, thank you, thank you!*

Roscoe and I went by the Gusano Club to meet Josefina's cowboy. We sat in a booth and Josefina grudgingly slammed two tequilas down on our table and flourished her bar rag, flicking some quartered limes into my lap. Roscoe and I had a good laugh at Josefina's high handed ways, especially since I knew for a fact that she was turning tricks on the side when the cowboy was on the road because I'd seen her, more than once, heavily made up, in a smart black dress showing lots of cleavage, going into the Palacio del Oro, directly across the street from the Gusano Club.

After a moment a tall, scraggly American in a JB Hunt shirt walked in and approached our table.

"Mind if I join y'all? Daryl Rivers. Whew! Twenty-one days out and three at home. Boy, I'm *tahrd!* I mean I'm *tahrd!* Man, you know that I-10 through Louisiana is easily the bumpiest stretch of major highway in America. It'll beat you to death in a cab over."

At the Navy Rose I questioned Felisa, over drinks in a booth, about Ysela. I managed to learn that Ysela was working at the Palacio de Oro, the Gold Palace, but that she was still in the relationship with the boxer. I had no intention of going to see Ysela anyway until I got a job. I wanted to walk into the Gold Palace with some money in my pocket. I wanted to treat Ysela royally, not just "go to the room."

Then Felisa told me this story: Felisa, her mother and Lucinda went to the Juárez Cathedral for Lucinda's Confirmation. Ysela and the boxer were supposed to join them, but they hadn't arrived. The three entered the church, crossed themselves, and Felisa and Monalisa sat down in a pew while Lucinda joined the other child candidates gathered in front of the priest. But something went wrong. There was an American. He was sitting near the front, and he was staring at Lucinda.

"An American? Who was he? Did you know him?"

"No."

"What did he look like?"

"*Muy feo*…very ugly." He was sweating profusely, she said. Balding, about forty-five, pudgy and a little drunk. He was licking his lips and looking over the children as if they were pastries in a bakeshop.

"Especially at Lucinda, he was staring, and he was sweating, sweating…"

Meanwhile, the priest had begun his litany: "Do you reject Satan and all his works and all his empty promises?"

The children answered in chorus: "I do."

The American was licking his lips, his eyes on Lucinda.

"Do you believe in God the Father Almighty, creator of heaven and earth?"

"I do."

The American kept squirming in his seat, and then he drank from a silver flask.

"Do you believe in Jesus Christ, His only Son, Our Lord, who was born of the Virgin Mary, was crucified, died, and was buried, rose from the dead, and is now seated at the right hand of the Father?"

"You should have seen Lucinda, her eyes, so big, so serious."

"I do…"

Then the ceremony ended, and as Felisa and Monalisa descended the stone steps of the cathedral with Lucinda in tow, the American stepped close behind them, panting like a dog. They tried to ignore him, but when they began walking along 16th of September Street the brute lurched forward and blocked their path.

"How much? How much for her?" He pointed at Lucinda. "How much for the little girl?"

"He was drunk, sweating like a filthy pig! He was sweating, sweating…"

The American reached in his pocket and held up a crisp one hundred dollar bill.

"How much for the little girl? *A como se vende?* How much?"

Lucinda cowered behind Felisa and began to cry. Monalisa stepped in front of Lucinda and stood shaking her fist at the man. Felisa spat in the American's face, and the three hurried away.

"Get out of here, you *guero* son of a bitch!" Felisa called over her shoulder.

The American, grinning, wiped the spit from his face

and waved the bill.

"Hey! Hey you!" he shouted. "I know you. You work at the Navy Rose Club. You're a whore! You're a whore!"

6

REYMUNDO DIED SHORTLY AFTER EASTER. He got sick. He got very weak. It happened suddenly. He started spitting up blood. When I heard about it I went to see him. He was lying on his bed in his stuffy room on *Calle Dr. M. Samaniego* above a tortilleria, attended by Paulo and Glorieta. He looked awful. He'd been spitting blood continually. The sheets and pillowcases were soaked. It had been going on all night. He was hemorrhaging inside. When I entered the room, he greeted me with a wink and a nod then sank back into his array of pillows. The effort of saying hello had exhausted him. His closed eyelids fluttered. He pressed a white handkerchief to his lips to sop up the blood that was seeping out.

Reymundo's room was a place to camp, nothing more. There was a dressing table and a mirror, a clutter of cosmetics. His outfits hung in the open closet, gauzy netlike dresses, stringy halters, blousy harem pants, slinky sweater sets, dainty things, sexy skirts no bigger than a bandana, lacy mantillas and ratty fur pieces complete with little paws and mummified faces of minks, even a bridal gown. Reymundo's room was more like a dressing room than a home. This was where he brought his sweethearts; this was the trysting-place, the longed-for citadel of his fastidious lusts; here was the bed where they writhed together in the delicious transports of love.

I'd never seen Reymundo without his makeup, the thick mascara and the eye shadow and the rouge that gave his toast-brown skin a warm peachy glow. Now his face was chalk-white, the bright lips like blood on snow, and the eyes, which had burned so feverishly, were faded and diminished, no longer seductive, but serene. The transformation was startling. He had already abdicated. What a lovely death it was, what an easy death. From his bloodstained pillow he smiled enigmatically, like some heraldic personage passing in a medieval show.

The priest arrived, smelling of incense and death, and in his wake Profunda, clutching her rosary, shrouded in a lacy black mantilla. She had on her war paint; she had to be at work in an hour or so. As she gazed silently at Reymundo and fingered her crucifix, tears welled up in her bulging brown eyes.

"*Tell me*," she demanded fiercely, clutching my arm. "*Digame, mi amor.*"

"Tell you what?" I said. "What are you talking about?"

"*Digame que no me quieres.* Tell me that you no have the love for me."

I realized that Profunda wanted me to release her, that she desired the death of her tortured infatuation for me.

"I don't love you," I whispered in Spanish, stroking her hair. "I cannot marry you."

Just then Paulo snorted and blew his nose. Glorieta was sobbing. Yet somehow it seemed altogether fitting and proper, as they say, that Reymundo should die in this stuffy little room above a *tortilleria*. A gorgeous moth was spreading its immense shimmering wings for the last time. The single window was open, the filthy curtain fluttered in the soft breeze. Reymundo raised his head and pressed the blood-soaked handkerchief to his bright lips. His wings were faintly vibrating. The life was going out of him. He was looking out at Mariscal Street for the last time, the shooting lights, the carnival sprawl. This was his world, the life he had lived to the hilt. Downstairs in the bakery, the women were rolling balls of dough, hovering over the *metate*, chattering like parrots, patting out tortillas. Beggars clustered outside, urchins pressed their snotty noses against the steamed window. Whores marched by, gaudy as jungle mammies, shouting cheerful obscenities at taxi drivers and pushcart vendors. On every street corner there was music and laughter. The cantinas were filling up with *braceros* and soldiers eager to get drunk. Mariachis, ready for another tussle, roamed the streets in predatory bands. The night was beginning.

Before it was over there was an argument between Paulo and Glorieta. Paulo wanted to take Reymundo to a hospital, but Glorieta insisted he shouldn't be moved. They'd called the doctor hours ago, but of course he hadn't arrived. Everything takes time in Mexico. Paulo wanted to call another doctor. Glorieta kept babbling about a certain *curandera* out in the Colonia Palo Chino who healed the sick by witchcraft. Paulo rushed out to a taco stand and called a taxi. He said he was taking Reymundo to the hospital regardless. Glorieta said he wouldn't permit it. It went on and on, a lot of fluttering and twittering, like two parakeets puffing up and batting their feathers, and while they were waiting for the taxi to take Reymundo to the hospital, he died.

7

SHORTLY AFTER REYMUNDO'S DEATH I too spread my wings. I fled Mariscal Street without a word to Profunda or Paulo or Roscoe or anyone. I flew to Los Angeles and perched in a loft in the warehouse district, where, for several months, I worked on a novel based on the letters I'd written for the girls on Mariscal Street. *Those crazy letters…* Title? *The Further Adventures of Fallopio* by Jerzy Mulvaney, of course.

When I'd done as much as I could on the manuscript, some innate homing instinct turned my feet back around toward Mother Juárez. I was sick of words. I wanted to hear Spanish spoken. I wanted to sit still and let life wash over me, in a stream unbroken by action, and especially by thought. I simply wanted to *be.*

But there was more to it than that. I had an *idea,* an idea that had begun to obsess me. It was the idea of "becoming a Mexican." I'd already lived in Mexico as an American, but this, what I had in mind, was different. It involved blending into the scenery. It involved relinquishing my language, my culture, my identity. I wanted to destroy and dissolve whatever remained of my identity, my *American* identity, and melt down into a primal, undivided being. Because the greatest thing is to be unknown, anonymous, free.

I arrived in El Paso on a Sunday evening. It was late November; Christmas was coming; half a year had passed. I checked my stuff in a bus station locker and walked across the bridge, plowing straight down Avenida Juárez to 16th of September Street, where enormous splashy billboards tilting off roofs of buildings created a cartoon motif.

I strolled down *Calle Ugarte*, on the fringe of the whore district. The cool night air was charged with the promise of rain. The stars were ringed with jagged haloes of orange-ice light. I arrived at Mariscal Street, and it was as if I were seeing it for the first time—the battered taxis, the goose-necked street lamps, the gutters choked with filth, the doors of the clubs yawning open, the painted faces of the women, their loose, smirking lips and smoldering oyster eyes.

A few steps further and the lopsided doorman at the Old West Club caught my arm and peered up into my face.

"Is it you, *guero?*"

"Hello, my friend. How have you been?"

"A girl is asking for you, *amigo*. For many months. She work at the Navy Rose Club. Can you buy me one tequila?"

After several drinks with the doorman, I made for the Navy Rose. The girl who'd been asking for me figured to be Profunda. I felt a twinge of guilt. I hadn't thought of Profunda in months. I hadn't even remembered to put her in the book. Why did she want to see me? Undoubtedly, she wanted me to write a final letter to the Colonel. Well, that was it. My guilt evaporated. Everything was coming up roses after all. I hadn't deserted Profunda, no, I was handing her a ticket to a new life. Profunda had finally seen the light. She was going to marry the little iron man, and more power to her. Profunda was going to pull off the butterfly trick. She was going to burst the silken bonds of her cocoon. She would spread her gossamer wings and fly away from Mariscal Street, the Boulevard of Broken Dreams, to a land flowing with milk and honey, and I had been instrumental in producing this moment of fruition, this moment of flight.

I walked through the swinging doors of the Navy Rose Club. The place was practically deserted except for Paulo, who was standing on a stepladder painting the ceiling. Paulo often did little chores around the place when things were slow.

There had been a change in Paulo since Reymundo's death. He looked graver, older, more like an afternoon bartender than a dancer. I watched Paulo slop some paint on the ceiling, flapping his arm like a huge flightless bird. He didn't move like a dancer at all. He was a little drunk, I noticed, as he turned and spotted me.

"*Cuñado*," he said, his eyes moistening with emotion. "You are back."

After we shook hands and embraced, he jerked his head toward the *cuartos*, the girls' rooms. "She wants you to write the letter."

"Profunda?" I muttered. "You mean to the Colonel?"

"*Sí*, she is going to marry him." Paulo spoke softly, gazing sorrowfully into my eyes.

"Jesus, that's great!" I said. "Hey, what's the matter, my friend? You act like it's a tragedy or something."

Paulo gave me a half smile, his oily pitted face spattered with drops of white paint. I noticed for the first time that his hair was going gray.

"She is getting out of here, man," he said shakily, squeezing my hand, almost in tears. "I never will."

I put my arm around his shoulders and hugged him. "You'll make it, brother," I said. "There's still time."

"No, *ese*," he said soberly. "For me it is over." He kissed me tenderly on the cheek.

I walked past the bar, pushed aside the torn curtain and paused in the narrow hallway that led to the girls' rooms. It was ironic to reflect that Profunda, of all the butterflies I knew on Mariscal Street—and many were stunning—that Profunda, with her ponderous dense body, should be the one to spread her wings and take flight.

I opened the door of Profunda's cell. She was sitting on the rumpled bed with her robe gathered loosely around her. Her hair was pinned up in curlers and she had a safety razor in her hand. She'd been shaving her legs. She looked at least ten years older.

There was no warm greeting as had been our custom. Silently and reproachfully, she pulled a crumpled five-dollar bill out of her bra and placed it on the brown bed sheet between her fat knees. Gazing at me, and through me, with the stony calm of a Neolithic goddess, she lit a *Farito* and blew the smoke in my face. Then she raised a hefty arm and began shaving her armpit, scraping at the black stubble with the dull blade.

"*Estás listo?*" she asked crisply. "Are you ready?"

"*Si, mi vida,*" I said meekly, poised with pen and paper.

"How do you say, *en Inglés,* '*Mi Querido Rafael, Chicitito,* My Baby Boy, My Darling, *Mi Amor, Mi Rafael Tan Guapo?*'"

"'Dear Ralph,'" I muttered.

"Okay, *bueno,*" she snapped, shooting me a venomous look. "Dear Ralph... It gives me the great happiness to marry for you *en este diez-y-seiz de Diciembre. Yo quiero mucho a ti, mi vida.* I will come to you on the *tren* with my *bebés...*"

8

IT WAS THE *desperateness* of Mexico that struck a chord in my soul. On the dilapidated buses, like the one that ran from Mariscal Street to Colonia Alta Vista, I saw men in rags, but proud and defiant; whereas in America a man in the same ratty condition is inevitably downtrodden, broken in spirit. The men I saw on the *colonia* buses were not derelicts; they were men who were desperately poor, outlaws almost, men walled in by poverty, men with nothing on the horizon, *pulque* drinkers, desperadoes, men up for anything—but *men.*

During this second Juárez period the Navy Rose Club—my Oasis in the American Desert—was fastening its tentacles around me like a soft, velvety octopus. America for me was now a land of myth ringing in the distance. In its place was Mariscal Street, the Boulevard of Broken Dreams, the street of the crooked smile and the practiced caress, the street of the warmth that is switched on and off like an electric light bulb. I'd forgotten all about Ysela during my stay in LA, or maybe I was trying to forget her now by plunging with a vengeance into the glitter-world of Mariscal Street. How many times, and with what puppy-like stupidity, I fell in love, and how many times, and how quickly, I was flayed alive and my hide flensed with an obsidian knife and hung up to cure in the sun!

There was a woman at the Navy Rose who at a certain hour of the night would drop the front of her gown and parade around bare-breasted on the balcony. It was like the climactic moment at a masquerade ball. Sometimes, later on, as the night was dying, "the Venus", as I called her, would come out in a pink robe, with her hair pinned up and cold cream on her face, and do a repeat performance. She'd fling the robe open, baring her splendid breasts. They were perfect *melones*, and she was obviously proud of their perfection. She hung out with another statuesque goddess—"Venus Number Two"—who looked very much like her. Both were handsome women, with strong features and beautifully decked out. They wore sausage-tight black dresses sparkly with sequins, long-stemmed black gloves, and, frequently, elaborate plumed hats that floated dreamily above their flawless complexions, arched eyebrows, beauty marks and kissy-wet lipstick. Both were extremely light in coloration; they were *gueras*, *blancas*. There was hardly a touch of the *mestizo*, no sugaring off into the indolent sensuality and melancholy of the Indian races. I would never have guessed either of them to be Mexican if I hadn't seen them in Juárez, Mexico, in the Navy Rose Club, standing on the balcony with their tits bared.

The two Venuses made a nightly circuit of the cantinas, hopping from bar to bar. In each, they'd bare themselves and go graciously through their act, then after lapping up the applause and adoration, they'd move on to center stage in the next cantina. Theirs was an enchanted existence. They were celebrities on Mariscal Street. Everywhere they went they were enthusiastically received. I know because often it happened that I was in another cantina when the magic hour of midnight arrived and the two made their entrance. On the balcony of the Palmeras Club, for example, and always as the night approached its climax, their appearance somehow inciting everything to rise to a crescendo. They had charisma, these two pagan goddesses. In their cold narcissistic fascination with their own bodies they symbolized the hard glittering passion of Mariscal Street, the pulse of the music, the drinks poured down the gullet, the glistening breasts and shining teeth of the love-dolls, the heat-damp-touch-throb excitement, the gut-level sex-joy, and the trumpets of the mariachis showering despair over it all. Their power to evoke all this was their function in life and their art.

Frequently, at the intersection of Mariscal and Calle Ugarte, a block from the Palmeras Club, an old man with a single red floating eye would be sitting in a folding chair, plucking a deep-bellied harp. A familiar figure, he hiked all through the whore district, lugging his folding chair and his golden street harp with little peg legs and a cigar box affixed to the graceful S-curved front pillar for catching coins. The luminous notes he released were golden threads that wove among the snippets of pork rind sputtering on the grills, the orange and yellow ears of corn and the halved papayas—gorgeous, inviting, like a woman's sex.

There was a whore spot near the Delicias Club with a big iron gate, and the walls were scarred like crumbling flesh. *Los Baños*, it was called. But there were no baths. The place reminded me of the Catacombs. Women, clothed in transparent shifts, pressed themselves against the iron grating, leaning out, jabbing with glowing cigarette tips, ogling passersby. "Pssst! Hey, Johnny! Suckie-fuckie? *No pagas mucho*. You no pay too much, Johnny."

While price was discussed and pleasantries exchanged, whore and prospective customer fondled each other through the bars like Pyramus and Thisbe, the imprisoned lovers of classical antiquity. If you arrived at a bargain, the iron gate was swung open and you followed the object of your lust—swinging her keys, clutching her roll of toilet paper—up two flights of rickety wooden stairs to one of the usual cell-like *cuartos* where the business was conducted.

The women at Los Baños were too old, too unattractive, or too unconfident to make it whoring in the cantinas. You didn't dance or buy drinks, as in the regular places. Here in the Catacombs, at Los Baños, I met Alicia Martinez. She was man-crazy. After our first interlude, she took me on for nothing, several times in fact, before I got to know her. After I got to know her, after I learned just how desperate her circumstances were, I insisted on paying. Sometimes I brought her money, not much, a few dollars now and then. I even got her a job at the Navy Rose, but she only stayed at the Rose for a few days, then she drifted back to Los Baños. Alicia wasn't pretty enough for the Rose, and on top of that she simply didn't have the confidence.

I'd stumble into Los Baños bloody drunk, just before dawn, after hitting all the other dives. The gate of the convent was of course locked, and the sisters had all retired, but I'd simply climb over the bars. I'd knock on Alicia's door. Sometimes she was with a customer, but usually she was not. She'd let me in—with a scolding, that is. She'd come to the door with a finger to her lips, in her preposterous tent-like nightgown, clutching a robe around her, like a respectable housewife, which at the bottom of her heart she aspired to be. If there happened to be a customer sprawled naked on the bed, waiting, with a hard-on pointing at the ceiling, she'd kiss me and murmur, "*Ay, mi amor. Ay, pobrecito,*" all the while gazing plaintively into my eyes, her own misting over, and shaking her head wistfully, a reference to my drunken state. "*No te vayas.* Don't go." And then: "*Hay voy,*" making the gesture with her thumb and forefinger held an inch apart, which in Mexico means, "In a minute..."

Alicia wanted to get married, and that scared me. I knew I couldn't support her, and besides, I wasn't in love with her. Alicia would have been overjoyed to be a housewife, to take care of her husband and her children, but fate had placed her behind iron bars. From the shadows she called out to young soldiers while the eerie glow of the pushcart man's brazier lit up her coarse features and the crumbling wall behind her.

We fell downstairs, or rather I fell downstairs, *bump-bump-bump*, on my heels-tailbone-heels-tailbone, laughing all the way and crashed sprawling on the landing below drawn up into the fetal position like a paratrooper exiting a plane, head down, legs extended, elbows tucked in at my sides. I was drunk and that was what saved me, as the saying goes. Alicia shrieked in horror and hurried down to get me. Another night the same thing happened, except this time she fell with me. We laughed until our sides split. What were a few bruises to the likes of me, and for a big strong girl like Alicia, falling downstairs was nothing. This was our one melting moment. She kept hugging and kissing me. "*Besame, mi amor,*" she murmured. "*Ay, mi amor, te quiero...*"

Braulia was in her late thirties, tired, but still beautiful. She had a resigned expression, saintly almost. She worked at the Delicias Club. She'd pretend not to notice while I did her, which I found exciting, because of the question which her performance or non-performance raised in my mind, that is, was she really as resigned, really as oblivious as she made out, or was she in fact secretly enjoying it? This was the question, the crux of our relationship. The almost-saintly aspect of her character made the whole thing seem rather ridiculous, which I found I liked. It *was* ridiculous, and at the same time it was super-sexed, because of the clandestine aspect. This was the lash that goaded me on. The expression on her face was the same as if she were running off a load of laundry, or perhaps praying, the eyes always averted.

Fucking Braulia was like violating a nun. I gave her fierce twists, in order to wake her up. I tried all sorts of stunts in order to get her to blow her cool. I handled her roughly, like a sack of potatoes. I flipped her like a pancake and fucked her upside down, bouncing her off the walls and ceiling, all of which caused her to close her eyes and turn down the corners of her mouth in self-righteous martyrdom. I wanted to throttle her, but I went about my business in a calm fury. I had paid my *dinero*, and by God I wanted the whole show. But Braulia stubbornly refused to acknowledge my presence, except to keep up a conversation about homemaking subjects, ironing, ways to save money, and her family, emphasizing the fact, it seemed to me, that she had grown children practically my age. Her son, for example, who, unlike me, was serious about life—he'd graduated from school, had a good job, he was married and settled and the rest of it. "He is in . . . *oof!*—Mazat—*oof!*—lan, at the—*ah!*—home of my—*ay!*—mother. He will return—*oof!*—for my—*oh, come on, baby!*—niece's—*ah!*—confir—*oof!*—mation!"

Elida, at the Gato Negro Club, much younger, was also "absent", but with Elida it was a different thing entirely. Her forces were shattered. She wasn't at all like Braulia, who was in complete control of herself—at least most of the time—yet both were equally remote. As for Elida, the first time I went to the room with her she was so gorgeous it was over before I noticed that she wasn't participating. On the next go-round, several nights later, instead of spending my four bucks in the usual way, I sat on the edge of the bed and tried to talk to her, holding her hand, which was rigid and lifeless, all the wrong words, romantic simpleton that I was, but I couldn't awaken her from her catatonic trance.

This was a phenomenon I frequently observed on Mariscal Street, very young girls who came to Juárez from little towns deep in the interior to make a killing, filled with romantic dreams of success or an exciting new life, never imagining the actual reality of it, and then the initial shock was enough to immobilize them. One wound and they retreated—for good. From this moment onward they were merely a body passed from hand to hand. Yet there were other girls, equally young, also from tiny pueblos deep in Mexico, who took swimmingly to the life on Mariscal Street.

In general there were three types. First, the hard, glittery ones, who might be very young, or not-so-young. They were completely cynical, materialistic, frequently very sexy. Apollo, the god of reason, ruled these statuesque women. They were cold, calculating, and often beautiful. They were the high-powered ones, the personality powered, thin-lipped, light in coloration, *blancas*, classic featured. Ice water flowed in the veins of these human dynamos whirling in a fizzing neon void. These women were what is sometimes referred to as a "cold mechanical fuck."

The second type were the earthy ones: sloppy, sentimental, self-indulgent. Wherever they happened to squat, they threw litters of babies: brown, chocolate, *café au lait*, who cares? They were superbly healthy specimens, large-boned, stocky or pudgy, full-breasted, the mouth generous, sensual, Polynesian, and along with it a jolly disposition which freely proclaimed their marvelous bovine health. Events such as pregnancies, births, and the inevitable succession of lovers rolled away from these women like water off a duck's back. Such women might actually be molded out of clods of earth. They were archetypal women who were as at home on Mariscal Street as they would have been on Bora Bora, or in the Stone Age. They emanated an organic intelligence. Frequently their coloration was dark, *morena* or *negra*. The Indian element was present, but not enough to make them melancholy or soulful. Their involvement with life was immediate. They enjoyed life, but with a certain thick-headedness and lack of passion that is characteristic of bovine people.

The third type were the girls who were vulnerable. They had a drop too much of Indian blood, which means sorrow, mysticism, and soul. Or a drop too much of

Spanish blood, which means fatalism, a destructive passion, an addiction to suffering, an obsession with death. Their first collision with the merciless glitter-world of Mariscal Street spelled disaster and retreat. They were schizophrenic. Their immediate experience was a movie that they viewed from the last row of an empty theater, enclosed in a schizophrenic twilight. The night I met Elida, the girl at the Gato Negro, there was a flash of recognition, as when two sleepwalkers meet in a darkened hallway. I wanted to enter her special schizophrenic twilight world and merge her dream with mine, but she wouldn't let me into her dream, and what I did with her body was of no concern to her, since she was no longer inhabiting that particular environment.

I never went to the room with Elida again, but frequently at the Gato Negro I bought her drinks and tried unsuccessfully to communicate with her. Her dress was dirty and her hair was matted and uncombed. While the *caballeros* mauled and kissed her, she sat with her hands rigidly folded in her lap, sometimes muttering a few disconnected phrases without looking up, frozen, obliterated, her pretty face murdered with cool plastic death. After she left the Gato Negro, I saw her once or twice at another club down the line, then, not at all. Evidently she'd been swallowed up, or had drifted off to join the ranks of the nameless ones who lurked in the shadows of the cold feathery trees by the crumbling stone steps of the cathedral on Diez y Seiz de Septiembre, near *La Calle Noche Triste*, the Street of the Sad Night.

9

AN INDIVIDUAL WHO, like Roscoe, was obsessed with returning to the womb, a man I often mentally compared with Roscoe, was the Clap Inspector. The Clap Inspector came by the Navy Rose Club frequently—the Clap Inspector and his accomplice. They were two elegant Toulouse-Lautrec dandies, real dudes with official-looking shiny black cases, knifing their way through the crowd, crisp, precise, devastatingly handsome in their shiny black suits, perfect diplomats, all the while gracefully overlooking our presence, that is, us, the patrons, the riffraff, and the bartender, Angel Mike—or Paulo, if it was afternoon—and the big-breasted *mesera* hurrying with her lacquered tin tray, and the girls, usually about fifteen of them, sprawled on the cushioned benches or sitting around the glowing jukebox which reminded me of a Nuremberg Stove, or leaning back insolently in their chairs, many of them half sloshed or crazed with a sense of personal melodrama, reeking of delicious perfume, painted to the gills, their faces wet with the many slavering kisses of their victims.

Always, after making their grand entrance, the Inspector and his henchman would march straight back past the *excusados* to one of the rooms where they'd set up shop, unpack their instruments and conduct examinations, give injections of penicillin and exterminate cases of crabs with the famous blue ointment. When they'd finished processing the girls, the pair, in their shirtsleeves, mopping perspiration, would emerge through the torn curtain that led to the cribs, with the same disdainful expressions on their mugs as before, like two tony-rich veterinarians who'd been emergency-called away from a fashionable party in Beverly Hills to inoculate a pigpen full of swine for hog cholera. They had the unmistakable air of men who had far better things to do. That they should have been obliged to perform such mundane chores was obviously an affront to their dignity.

It was laughable. The moment the two of them walked in the door of the Navy Rose Club everybody would get on their best behavior. The rowdy conversation at the bar would hush, the squeals of delight would die away as the couples feverishly pawing one another in the booths became more discreet, and nobody played the jukebox. After the elect had chosen their table, frequently evacuating the soldiers or *braceros* that were slouched around it, they'd order drinks, and Angel Mike and the buxomy *mesera* would move like puppets dancing on strings. Sometimes the Inspector would snap open his black attaché case and take out a manila folder and jot something down in a crisp neat hand. They acted like they were sitting on a starlit terrace in Barcelona sipping ices through a straw. Cool as a couple of flamingoes, these two jamokes. They were pleasantly blotto, going through the motions, and we didn't matter at all; we didn't exist, except subliminally, as atmosphere.

The Inspector himself was an aloof, calculating presence. With his crisply trimmed mustache and severe black coat he made me think of a photograph I once saw of the young Sigmund Freud, snapped during his student-prince days in Vienna. Often as I studied this perfectly barbered and manicured picture-book man I found myself wondering, what sort of a restaurant will he be dining in tonight, what'll he drink, and what sort of a doll will he be wearing on his arm? Everything spit and polish for this man, everything carte blanche, everything cool, crisp, collected. Not the tusked stupor of the unwashed, no wallowing in the mud, no rooting around among the turnips, nothing sleazy about this man, no sir. This guy was the Grand Tamale, the number one Rat-Bastard Impresario, and no mistake about it. The pair of them, the Inspector and his shadow, were like two who had come to us from a distant world, like Dante and Virgil descending into the realm of the dead.

There was one flaw with the Clap Inspector—he had a high girlish voice that betrayed his marvelous good looks. He was prissy. One night his shadow, who ordinarily was almost as prim and proper as the Inspector, hanging on his every word like a lapdog, one night this non-person, this nonentity, got drunk and hired the mariachis, one of the least successful and most predatory groups, Los Pájaros, a sinister, swarthy band of desperadoes whose clothing was grimy and tattered. It was rumored that they rolled drunks. They were doped-up, smelly, evil-looking, and at least half of them were carrying knives. The Inspector, who'd just returned from the toilet, took one look at these angels of doom huddled around his drunken, hiccupping subordinate and went into shock. Outraged to the core, he quickly gathered up his papers and chucked them inside his shiny black briefcase and snapped the case shut. But after a moment he hesitated, muttered something into his mustache, then primly sat down and glanced nervously at his watch through seven or eight choruses of "Viva Chihuahua", while the musicians, wise to his discomfort, enjoyed themselves hugely, winking at everyone, flashing their gold teeth, deliberately prolonging the number, and we all had a good laugh at the Inspector's expense.

Always, after the two of them finally settled their bill and prissed out the door, a huge tide of relief surged through the Navy Rose, and every girl had a band-aid on her calf or thigh, which meant she'd just been shot full of penicillin and was probably a safe bet, at least for a few days, but I've known girls in all the Mexican border towns to stick a band-aid on their leg for that very reason (*but that's Mexico*) so one can never be sure.

The Clap Inspector, like Roscoe, I conjectured, was obsessed with returning to the womb, and at the same time, like Roscoe, he despised women, because of his obsession, because of the power the obsession had over him. And no exaggeration, because it, his obsession, determined his career and the course of his life. That is, he spent eight hours a day, six days a week, peering into the cunts and cavernous gaps of the most frequently-fucked women in Mexico, the butterflies of Mariscal Street.

The Inspector was the priestly figure of Dante invested with the arrogance of the gynecologist. He acted as though his profession were a religious office, as if to say, "*I alone may part the veil.*"

I often pictured him on his knees in the dirty room and the woman lying on the rumpled, soiled bed, with her legs pulled up. He blinks his eyes then, with his fingers, spreads the little lips. He pokes his pencil flashlight gadget inside and shines it around like a miner, like a glowworm timidly peering into a churning factory of flesh creation. *There* is where he'd like to be. *Flamingo Heaven!* Why did he ever leave? Stupid, wasn't it? It was so much better in there, so pink, so fleecy, so safe, and so warm. *This* is the garden planted eastward in Eden, *this* is the gate guarded by the Cherubim and the flaming sword. The fruit of the Tree of Knowledge is bitter, bitter. How much better to have eaten of the Tree of Life. What a mistake, what a monumental mistake. *Right garden, wrong tree!* Ruefully, he plucks a hair out of his mustache, in the manner of a man to whom all is lost. Lost, Flamingo Heaven, gone in a flurry of pink wings. Gone, the magical garden, the tiny enclosed world whose horizons he once touched with his fingertips. Sick at heart, filled with inexpressible longing, he adjusts his flashlight beam, he makes a crisp notation in his ledger. "*La vida no vale nada.*" *All for nothing!* If only he could crawl back inside, if only he could retreat back through the portals from which he emerged, to a land filled with myth, to that pink and fleecy land planted eastward in Eden, beyond the flaming sword which turns every way, forever protecting the Tree of Life.

10

"WHATEVER IS IMPERFECT IN AN ANGEL, let us ascribe to the angel's multiplicity." Somehow this line from Pico Della Mirandola seems to fit one girl in particular. She was really scrumptious; I was crazy about her. Her name was Maria Elena and she worked at a rat hole called the Noches de Oro, the Golden Nights Club. They called her "*La China*" because her eyes were slanted. Possibly she did have some Chinese blood. She was beautiful, beautiful. Just how many golden nights I spent with this angel I can't tell you, but it wasn't just "going to the room," as they say. We danced, we went to the movies and I took her to dinner at the Marfino Restaurant on Avenida Juárez, in the "nice" part of town, and it was wonderful. She was a wonderful girl, Maria Elena, but there was a catch, there was a "but." She had the clap. She had gonorrhea and by this I mean to say that she always had it, even though, like all of the girls on Mariscal Street, she was regularly inspected and shot full of penicillin, and the reason she always had it was because what she had was a particularly resistant strain of the famous Juárez clap.

Thus it was Maria Elena who led me to Dr. Umberto. I kept going back to the Noches de Oro, back to Maria Elena, and I kept getting infected then re-infected, so I'd go to Dr. Umberto, who shot me up with penicillin.

Dr. Umberto, "the Clap Doctor," was a very interesting man. He was from Argentina but spoke English without a trace of an accent. He was fluent in six languages and read Latin and Greek. He was also a free-fall parachutist, a jet pilot, a cordon-bleu chef and a member of Mensa, the high-hat organization for intellectuals. A short man, around 5'4", plump yet sleek as a barracuda, he had such energy and such charisma that he seemed much larger physically than he was. Shockingly handsome and absolutely irresistible to women, he positively filled the room with his sleek, sweetly dangerous presence.

"*Barracudesque*" is the adjective I coined to describe Dr. Umberto.

Dr. Felix Umberto wasn't your typical rich doctor. He had no nurse, his office was in his home near Concordia Cemetery, and he drove an old beat-up type E Jaguar. After I'd gone to Dr. Umberto many times for inoculations, and he learned that I was a writer and that I was passionately interested in ideas, we began having long conversations, sometimes talking far into the night, and frequently I'd end up staying over. One thing led to another and finally he invited me to join his household and serve as a sort of factotum, gentleman's gentleman and amanuensis. I suppose he realized that I wasn't going to pay my bill.

I wasn't the only one, by any means. It was a huge house and several other refugees were also camping with Dr. Umberto, most of them, like me, victims of genitourinary calamities. The retired Israeli machine gunneress with the prolapsed uterus, for example: she dropped her intestines in the toilet one morning. I never heard a more agonized scream come from a human throat, and that's the bloody truth. She was very attractive. Oddly enough, I never tackled her, even though her room was right across the hall from mine. To tell you the truth, I was leery of it. A woman like that could fall apart on a man.

This, then, was the beginning of my period of indentured servitude at Dr. Umberto's. My chores included feeding the cats and changing their litter boxes, bathing the leaves of the rubber plants with milk, feeding the fish, typing, taking dictation, and occasionally cooking a meal, as well as sweeping up around the place.

I will tell you that I was the only one among the inmates at Dr. Umberto's who pitched in at all. The rest of them didn't do jack shit. The other squatters (excluding the machine gunneress, who wasn't with us for long) were dullards, nothings, middle-aged fogies. Not a live one in the lot. (I hope you're reading this, my former playmates!)

But I don't mean to sound ungrateful. Room, board and free penicillin shots: I had myself a pretty sweet deal.

Raul was an exception—Raul from Argentina, Dr. Umberto's nephew. I almost forgot about him. Raul was with us for a few days. A cheerful and willing worker, Raul was at first glance a dead ringer for Dr. Umberto—short, sleek, rounded, beaming—but once you got to know him you realized that he was somehow second rate, a body double, a simulacrum, almost—a preliminary sketch, even—of the great man, as if life could create this brilliance—the diamond-like sparkle of Dr. Felix Umberto—only once.

In the waiting room, huddled patiently as I made my rounds, were women with grimy babies on their laps, wrapped in shawls, hawking and spitting into crumpled handkerchiefs, and scowling toddlers with runny noses, and the men, young and old, unshaved, slouched like zombies in the stiff plastic chairs, muttering their lepers' prayers. They were the poor who lived lives of quiet desperation in the barrios of El Paso. These souls comprised about half of Dr. Umberto's patients. The other half were middle-class matrons who were in love with him. As for the poor, Dr. Umberto patched them up and sent them on their way. If they were able to pay him something, then fine and dandy; if not, he didn't press them. Kindness was one of the qualities Dr. Umberto possessed in abundance. He exuded kindness like a platypus exuding milk through its pores.

Soon after I moved in the good doctor put me on his pet project, a book he had in progress, a book entitled *Short Men in History*. *Short Men in History* was a study that purported to show that throughout recorded history an overwhelming number of men who did great things or lived great lives were—like Dr. Umberto himself—short men. But he was having problems with the book. Dr. Umberto was good at amassing data, but when it came to presenting it he fell somewhat flat in that his writing was excessively academic. It was a strange thing... When Dr. Umberto talked he was brilliant, but when he sat down at the typewriter invariably his voice flew out the window. "If only you would write the way you *talk*," I often said to encourage him, but somehow he couldn't seem to do that. So, my job was to take the manuscript and goose it up, punch it up a little bit, inject some life into it. In addition, when Dr. Umberto discovered that I was a good hand with the research, I was dispatched to the library on a weekly basis to ransack the history books for likely subjects for his study. Evenings we'd get together around the pool table with cigars and a bottle of Tia Maria and we'd go over my findings.

"What have you got for me?"

"Let me see…Napoleon five-two, James Madison five-four, Geronimo five-five, Picasso five-two and a half…"

"Good, good!"

"Julius Caesar five-two, Lawrence of Arabia five-three, Phil Sheridan five-four, Billy the Kid five-three...and, get this, you're gonna love this one, *Jefe*. Ready?"

"Ready!"

"Ghandi four-eleven..."

"Ghandi four-eleven? Yeah, good! Nice work!"

"And Attila the Hun was a dwarf. Did you know that, *Jefe?*"

I don't remember exactly when I started calling Dr. Umberto "*Jefe*." I mean, he wasn't my boss, he was my friend, but I called him "*Jefe*," just joking around, and the name stuck.

"A dwarf! A dwarf, you say. No, I didn't. I didn't know that. What about Pepin the Short?"

"Pepin the Short? He was short, *Jefe*. That's all I've—"

"Short? Of course he was short. But how short? That's the question."

"I haven't been able to turn up anything."

"The hell with it then. Just fill it in yourself. Get something down on paper. Think outside of the box, man!"

"You want me to do that?"

"Sure!"

"Okay, Pepin the Short, five-four."

"Shorter than that."

"Five-two."

"Yes! I like that! Pepin the Short, five-two. That's good, that's really good..."

One afternoon I was sprinkling fish food on the limpid surface of the water in the aquarium when Dr. Umberto entered the living room with an elegant, gazelle-like white woman in tow. Very tall, she towered over *El Jefe*.

"This is Tizanzia DeForrest-Gallant," he announced. "She's writing a book about her family. Her mother, a Philadelphia debutante, married a Russian count. The lousy bastard sold her into slavery, and she subsequently spent fifteen years in a Siberian gulag."

"Nice to meet you," I managed.

"Let's go into the kitchen," Dr. Umberto continued. "I'm making my special *gambas al ajillo*, garlic prawns. I thought we could all have lunch."

Tizanzia DeForrest-Gallant and I sat at the kitchen table drinking vermouth on the rocks with a twist of lemon as we watched Dr.Umberto mince and sauté the garlic.

"Felo, that smells heavenly!" Tizanzia DeForrest-Gallant exclaimed.

"Let's have some wine, shall we?" Dr. Umberto held up a bottle. "Marques de Riscal Rioja Tempranillo. The Tempranillo grape produces a wine with a dusty, leathery edge to its raspberry and blackberry fruit tones. This particular Tempranillo goes wonderfully with Roncal."

"Roncal?"

"Roncal, yes. Roncal is a creamy white sheep's milk cheese with subtle olive and pine nut nuances. Made only in certain remote mountain villages in the Pyrenees. Er, would you excuse me for a moment?"

Dr. Umberto left the room. Tizanzia DeForrest-Gallant and I finished off the bottle of Marques de Riscal and I opened another one.

"Tell me about Mexico," Tizanzia DeForrest-Gallant began.

"Mexico…sure. Mexico is the land where the sun always shines. Everything is copasetic in Mexico."

"Copasetic?"

"Yeah, copasetic. You know, *simpatico*."

"Go on, please."

"Mexico is the land where doves weep and even the stones have stories to tell…"

"The stones…stories? I like that."

"Yes, beautful, isn't it? And so convenient. *El baño?* This way, *Señorita*. Hangover? Menudo, of course. Menudo is the answer."

"Menudo?"

"Right, menudo. *Tripas*. Tripe. The cow's stomach. *Estómago*. Sympathetic medicine, you see. Sympathetic meaning *simpatico*, copasetic."

"Fascinating! You know what? I'm fucking wasted."

Just then Dr. Umberto popped back into the kitchen with a loaf of crusty French bread under his arm.

After a sumptuous lunch of garlic prawns and French bread, washed down with plenty of Marques de Riscal,

Tizanzia DeForrest-Gallant excused herself and toddled off to the rest room.

"Genital herpes, *cervicitis* and a touch of *chlamydia*," Dr. Umberto muttered in a cautionary tone, leaning close to my ear. "I wouldn't…"

"Don't worry!"

After I'd been living at Dr. Umberto's for some time I began to see him as my exact opposite. It may have been, at least partially, because I was rereading Dostoevsky's *The Double* at the time. In any case, it was uncanny but true. It was like gazing into a mirror and seeing myself upside down. Dr. Umberto was my opposite number: he was the successful man of the world, I was the misfit. As my opposite, he embodied all that was missing from my psyche, and quite a chunk it was, too. Is it any wonder then that I felt at times like a vapor? I was constantly besieged with the sensation that I might evaporate or simply blow away in a strong breeze. There was also the sensation of being invisible. In the street, I found myself checking for my reflection in storefront windows to make sure there was actually someone there. It was even sometimes almost as though Dr. Umberto might have imagined me, the startling thought that I was perhaps nothing more than a figment of his imagination. Dr. Umberto, on the other hand, my upside-down fraternal twin—this pudgy little man with hairy forearms sticking out of starched shirtsleeves, gold fabricated watchband composed of tiny interlocking squares, sly brown eyes like the eyes of an intelligent raccoon—he was perfectly solid, solid as a rock, he was too solid. He'd sit there, at the kitchen table—where our discussions usually took place— dense, thick, comfortably rounded, beaming at me like a Gouda cheese.

He was always asking me what I thought of him, *really*. One night I was standing at the ironing board in the kitchen drinking Tia Maria and pressing his tux pants with a damp washcloth. Wife Number Three had blown in unexpectedly from Buenos Aires. They were going to a shindig at the Hilton.

"Tell me," he entreated, standing there bare-legged on the cracked linoleum in his black silk socks and garters, plus his tux jacket, bow tie and boutonniere, "what do you think of me—*really?*"

"You're an arrogant little prick."

"Ah! An...arrogant little...*prick*. *Arrogant*, you say. *Fascinating!* An arrogant...little...prick. Hmm, yes..."

At odd moments he'd insist on a round of ping-pong, which for me was the *peine forte et dure*. While he drubbed me unmercifully he'd keep up a steady stream of intellectual patter, not strictly patter, either, but professorial discourses on the most abstruse subjects, such as the question of whether or not a certain atomic particle was charged with negative or positive ions. He was a recognized expert in a dozen fields and held fanatically strong opinions. He drove his points home with vicious slams of the paddle, smacking the ball into my face or chest while I strained my comprehension to the limit and tried clumsily to defend myself. It was frustrating and humiliating to say the least. Frequently, I was almost in tears.

There's one other thing that I should mention before we go on: the recurring attacks of malaria to which Dr. Umberto was subject. It was something he'd picked up in the jungle. It would hit him suddenly—chills, and then he'd be in bed for two or three days with a high temperature, completely delirious. My job when this happened was to look after him and see that he got his medication.

As for my health, it was perfect, thanks to the magic of penicillin. Maria Elena had long since run off with a Pepsi driver and I'd completed the work on Dr. Umberto's book, so there was really no reason for my staying on except that I liked Dr. Unberto immensely and I had every reason to believe that he felt the same about me.

One day after recovering from a bout of malaria, and after thrashing me at ping-pong, humiliating me at the pool table and wiping the floor with my ass at chess, he summoned me to his office to kill a spider. Just to see what he'd do, I refused. He reacted, as I might have predicted, with his usual logical thoroughness.

"Ah! You refuse. That's very interesting. Let's take a moment, shall we, to consider. Have a cigar? Fascinating, isn't it? Now, let me ask you something, a question, no, a series of questions. First of all, why...do you say no? But— one moment, please, before you answer. I am going to give you a partial list of possible motivations on your part, in the order that they occur to me—"

But here was one of the few times I got the better of Dr. Umberto. Halfway through his discourse, I squashed the spider.

11

I STARTED OUT TALKING ABOUT MARIA
ELENA, my angel from the Golden Nights Club, but it's
Ysela I should have been talking about all this time, not
Maria Elena. It's Ysela who was my real angel. It was Ysela
who brought me home to myself. I was merely in love with
Maria Elena.

Ysela had left the Gold Palace and worked now at La
Posada de Los Indios, on *Calle M. Martinez*, the cantina
with the giant molded Cruz Blanca bottle on top, near the
canal. The "Bottle Club" is what everyone called the place.

Ysela had a tattoo—a tarantula—on her left shoulder
blade. When I first saw Ysela's tattoo, the past came
rushing back—my childhood. As a child I adored spiders.
At the age of eight, I devoured Jean-Henri Fabre's *Life of
the Spider*, and subsequently, a biography of Jean-Henri
Fabre himself. I was fascinated by the sparkling portrait of
a serene old man, radiantly alive, sitting in his garden in
Provence contemplating nature. I was the same sort of
being, contemplative, precocious, prematurely old. Then I
was catapulted into the world. The result was disaster. The
precocious, contemplative child-sage showed little aptitude
for marching in step, firing point-blank, lobbing grenades,
reading a compass, driving a semi, teaching remedial

English, selling refrigerators, hawking chocolate pies, writing software-user manuals, bouncing drunks, repairing roller skates, decorating cakes, embalming corpses, throwing pizzas, hanging sheet rock, cleaning swimming pools, performing bladder irrigations, picking grapes, pumping gas, and working ineffectually at over two hundred other occupations. A failure! A flop. A misfit, a dreamer, a dud, a displaced person.

Then I met Ysela and I *remembered*. Once again I was the man I could have been, the man I might have been, the man I should have been. It was Ysela who restored this in me. It was she who brought me back to ground zero, to the true source of my being. I can't help quoting another French author I encountered later on in life. Here is Antoine de Nervèze in *Les amours de Filandre*:

"In her I saw the myth, the fable, all the fabulous invention and interweaving of detail that makes up the literature of escape—the quest for the grail, the lure of far-off lands, the voyage through uncharted seas, the great leaps of consciousness, the great leaps of faith, the heroic endeavors, the miraculous discoveries, the far-flung peoples, the forgotten languages, the secret rituals, the transcendent ideas, the aura and ambiance of worlds remote in time and worlds perhaps entirely imaginary, imaginary beings, imaginary lives, imaginary loves. Everything that our age does not contain I saw in her."

Ysela was deeply religious, and she was nuts about astrology, past lives, anything to do with the occult. She claimed that in another life she had been Carlota, the mad Empress of Mexico. Before that, a sorceress. But she had abused her power. She'd done evil. She likened herself to a spider that devours its mate. What Ysela believed, she believed absolutely. In her incarnation as the ill-fated Carlota, she'd faced madness and a firing squad. Now she was a whore. Her life was a journey of penance, of expiation. It was fate. She accepted her fate—her incarnation—with stoic courage. She didn't question the rightness, the cosmic legality, because she felt—and here, at least, I concurred—that this was not her province. Ysela's resignation to her life of penance left her free to do as she pleased. She was free to indulge herself completely, and without guilt, because she was already doing hard time. "The condemned ate a hearty meal." That was Ysela.

Our room...it was Ysela's room, actually, a rabbit hutch on the second floor of a crumbling adobe building a few doors north of the Bottle Club, paid for by Ysela's *novio,* the middleweight boxer Juan "El Indio" Mendoza, whose posters were plastered on buildings all up and down Avenida Juárez and throughout the red light quarter. Ysela and the pug were presently on the outs and I was hoping that things stayed that way, which seemed quite likely since Mendoza was a celebrity and had dozens of ladies.

When Pilar learned that her sister was seeing "that *callejero,*" as she called me, she was furious, but Felisa, who had recently migrated from the Navy Rose to the Bottle Club, was somewhat more welcoming. One night at the Bottle Club I bought Felisa a *copa* and we danced.

"Poor little guy," she murmured. "You've fallen in love with my sister! You poor, poor baby!"

Besides, I was no longer a *callejero.* I had a job now, busting suds at a Chinese restaurant, and I was living at Dr. Umberto's. I was getting serious about life, and I had my sights set on Ysela, even if I had to duke it out with Juan "El Indio" Mendoza.

Ysela... I brought her presents, perfume, flowers, candy and *Doctor Corazón* comic books. At the Bottle Club we spent hours writing out the words to jukebox songs on paper napkins, in English and Spanish. Yes, I was in love, and I began to look back now on our brief meeting that day at the makeshift temple of the Virgen de la Soledad in Colonia Alta Vista as both the beginning of something and the end of something. For me it was the end of the cowboy days, the freewheeling Roscoe days, and the beginning of an obsession.

We had fun. I'd bail her out of the Bottle Club for the night. If you wanted to take a girl with you, to a hotel, for example, you had to pay the house a "ransom" fee. I think it was ten dollars. So I'd ransom Ysela out and we'd go to the movies, the matinee, and then to dinner at the Marfino Restaurant on Avenida Juárez, for the *cabrito*, simmered with wine, lime, jalapeño and avocado, and served on banana leaves.

The movies are different in Mexico, different from America, I mean, and the whole experience is different, especially when you go to the matinees. I don't mean the avant-garde stuff, the Mexican *film*, Luis Buñuel and Hector Alejandro Galindo, I mean the *movies*, the cheap everyday fare that's dished up in movie theaters throughout Mexico. The impossibly idealized Mexican mother saying her beads and wringing her hands, weeping like a Madonna. *As if she was made out of candy!* Weeping for her son Pepe, slain in the taco alleys. *The tears!* The weeping and wailing that goes on.

In Mexico you pay a few pesos to go into a darkened theater and cry your eyes out, just like you go to the priest for absolution, to get it all off your chest. It's worth twelve and a half cents on the dollar to be able to cry, to let it all out. In Mexico, in the afternoons, at the matinees, there's never a dry eye in the theater. The lights come on, the hankies come out, everybody blows their nose and everyone looks at everyone else with red streaming eyes. Not shamefaced looks, not embarrassed looks, but rather, "*Tan triste, no?* Jesus, wasn't that sad? Let's have another one!" In Mexico, in the afternoons, the theaters are packed. Everybody loves the movies in Mexico. Here's where you see the young girls in their immaculate dresses, after they've sipped their ices in the cafés and flirted with the *caballeros*. In Mexico, even the *señoritas* love to have a good cry. *Que bonito es llorar!* It's good to cry. It's good for the soul.

And not only the *señoritas*, but the ladies of the night.

The whores all go to the movies in Mexico. It's a regular thing. They come straggling into the matinees in twos and threes, all gussied up, reeking with delicious perfume, in order to relax for an hour or two before going to work in the cantinas. I mean gals with ice water in their veins, women who lie there like a pine board while you fuck them, with their eyes rolling up dollar signs. They sit in the theater and they cry themselves silly over the most sodden episodes of impossible saccharine rapture. And they enjoy it! No Victor Hugo tugging the puppet strings here, as in America. No cosmic irony, no cold white marble statues that can't speak, and no vulcanized monster suits with ice cream epaulets because in Mexico the monster is at large, on the loose. So why the masks, I'd like to know, why the edelweiss strings pulled by the masters of drama from the balcony? Why not simply let it out, why not pull the stops, let it gush, let it go, flood the aisles, sink the theater, flood the world with tears? But that won't get it. Not in America. In our world, even a darkened theater, having paid the price of admission, you mustn't allow yourself to weep. If you should burst into tears, if you began to sob uncontrollably—particularly, say, in the middle of a musical comedy—why, they'd drag you out, just the same as if you'd molested somebody.

One night after drinks at the Gusano Club we had Ysela's picture taken sitting on a street photographer's wooden horse, a splendid striding black animal with white shanks, a horse so slim and regal that the photographer, in his drab brown Ike jacket, seemed as insignificant as a sparrow. I couldn't help thinking how exhilarating it would be to sit in the saddle of this handsome, spunky prancer with its silver concho-studded bridle and be wheeled through the streets of Ciudad Juárez like a benevolent monster. As I gazed up into Ysela's eyes I sensed that she was thinking the same thing, and for a crazy instant I seemed to see the mad Mexican empress Carlota mounted sidesaddle on the photographer's horse, naked as Lady

Godiva, her glorious hair awash, giggling and drooling while *braceros* and tourists pelted her with mango rinds and lottery tickets.

Ysela bit like a vampire, often drawing blood. My shoulders, chest and thighs were riddled with wounds, as though I'd been crawling through barbed wire. My back was scored with welts and scratches from her nails. Our lovemaking was frenzied. She was the hottest woman I ever encountered. Afterwards, while her eyes brimmed with tears, she would rumple my hair and call me *mocoso*, snot-nose.

Near our bed on a rickety stand was a water pitcher. The water cooled as it evaporated through the porous clay. Our window looked out on the sprawl of Mariscal Street, the bridge, the clotted green canal, a jumble of roofs and shanty taco stands, and a few ragged street dogs that prowled like hyenas. The veldt began at the windowsill.

There was a parrot in a cantina two doors north, the Toluca Club. He'd rattle his cage and croak, "You want a *weeskey*, Señor?" It went on at all hours of the day and night. That parrot never seemed to sleep.

We had plates brought up. It costs very little in Mexico. We'd throw the scraps out the window to the dogs, and sometimes we'd pelt merrymakers woozing their way home in the bleary hours of the morning, which was when we had our dinner. Then we'd go to bed, awakening in the afternoon as the cathedral bells tolled and the breeze ruffled the curtains. We'd make love again, then we'd send out for breakfast and Ysela would get ready to go to work at the Bottle Club.

I went with Ysela to the boxing matches. She said she wanted to give "El Indio" his ring back. I didn't believe her, but I went with her that night to the Coliseo and she met the pug backstage after his event. I talked with the boxer's seconds, or whatever they were now, nasty little characters with Zen-like mustaches of Eskimo shamans or dangerous mystical karate types. I was feeling pretty antsy.

In spite of what I said earlier about duking it out with Mendoza, I didn't relish the idea of swapping punches with a guy who spends eight hours a day in a gymnasium practicing how to kill people with his fists.

This was a pattern with Ysela. Right after her initial fling with Juan "El Indio" Mendoza, there was a picador, and after that a full-fledged matador. There were several bullfighters in her recent past and even a hockey player. She posed a series of dashing rivals who outdid me, hoping to incite my jealousy, but my love was steady, like a flame.

One of her tricks had to do with the framed autographed photo of Juan "El Indio" Mendoza she kept on a stand next to our bed. When things were going well I'd stick the photo in a drawer and she wouldn't bother to get it out. But if she was pissed off, or wanted to incite me to violence, she'd get the photo of the boxer out and prop it up again, and I had to stare at the palooka while we were making love.

She insisted, too, on telling me about her other men, every detail. She claimed she had to get it off her chest. The performance became a sort of ritual. About her infidelities, I mean. When I declined to become involved in the melodrama—that is, when I neglected to interrogate her, to rave, to rant, to smash the furniture—she became angry.

Roscoe conveniently fell in love with Marta, Ysela's *compadre* and *buena amiga* at the Bottle Club. We had a fabulous fling. We were delirious over our new *novias*. We went everywhere, double-dating, all over town, we did it up, full-on, while the glow lasted. Roscoe had somehow inveigled a loan from Beneficial Finance. He'd managed to borrow two thousand dollars. It was hilarious. I'm certain they're still chasing him.

Marta was pudgy and full of sass, like a Vienna sausage. She was plump, rounded, Polynesian-earthy. She came from Mazatlan. One night she tried to put the make on me. While Roscoe was waltzing around the dance floor with one of the other damozels, Marta dragged me back to her room. She pulled down the front of her dress. Her breasts were flaccid, pointed like mangoes. She had wads of toilet paper stuffed in her bra. She didn't try to hide it. We were sitting on the bed. She kissed me and unzipped my fly. Her lips tasted like stale Mexican cigarettes, *Faritos*. When nothing much happened she gave up the idea. But as a foursome we really clicked. Every night it was dinner and dancing. The best of everything, thanks to good old Beneficial Finance.

Ysela began putting on weight. She was looking better and better. I'd pat her belly, as if she were pregnant. We went to the movies, the bullfights, the nightclubs. When Roscoe and I were away from our sweethearts, we didn't go to the cantinas as before. Instead we'd have a quiet drink at the Gusano Club or the Rosita where we'd hash over our plans for the forthcoming night, like Pinocchio and Lampwick at Pleasure Island. Pilar was on the warpath, of course, but Roscoe gave her a few bucks now and then to keep her at bay. Just the same, I was plenty nervous because once when Pilar was drunk she'd talked about hiring an assassin—not all that expensive in Mexico—to dispatch both her wayward husband and his *callejero* friend.

My Dr. Umberto period came to an end, as all good things must. The completed "Short Men in History" manuscript was at the publisher's, the svelte, gazelle-like Tizanzia DeForrest-Gallant had been cured of her ills, and the two of them, she and Dr. Umberto, were off to Spain and Italy for an extended holiday.

I got a job and moved into a room in El Paso. The job was peeling posts. I worked with Johnny Caruthers, a feisty old man, and Ernest Peebles, a handsome young guy, very structured, moral, upright and precise, who was studying to become an X-ray technician.

Johnny Caruthers, our straw boss, chewed Beechnut

tobacco and rolled his own cigarettes. Johnny always had a drop of sweat poised at the tip of his nose and it would fall on the hand rolled cigarette that was perpetually glued to his lips. Johnny Caruthers worked like hell and he talked a blue streak.

We had to peel the posts and then lower them with a chain hoist into a creosote bath. To peel the posts, two workers with drawknives would stand at opposite ends of a post balanced on sawhorses and pull away from each other across the sawhorses. It takes time to get the rhythm. To break the monotony we'd change partners every once in a while.

Ernest Peebles was very energetic and applied himself to the hilt. He was the perfect worker. But Johnny Caruthers led the work, even though he was more than three times our age, easily seventy. Johnny was forever bragging about his youthful sexual encounters, in a way that put Ernest Peebles on edge. The encounters invariably seemed to take place in cars or trucks, and somehow the steering wheel, the clutch pedal and the emergency brake were always intimately involved.

"I got her right down under the steering wheel with her head on the clutch pedal, and one leg up there on the gearshift..."

Ernest didn't care at all for this kind of talk, and I wasn't exactly crazy about it either. It wasn't so much that it was "dirty," but it was *wearisome*. So we ganged up on Johnny Caruthers and ragged him unmercifully.

"You're too old, Johnny. Who gives a shit about an old fuck like you? You're going to die soon. You're nothing. How could you give a girl a thrill? What about the shit on your shirt and the tobacco juice stains? You don't amount to anything. You never did and you never will. You're an ignorant Mick, that's what you are. Just shut your fucking trap. Shanty Irish trash! Don't talk to us. Go ahead and report me to the boss. You think I give a fiddler's fuck?"

And so Johnny Caruthers became subdued. He stopped

his spouting of his past sexual encounters. When a little bit of it surfaced we'd cap it off, or Ernest did. But I felt bad. We had shut this man down all because of Ernest Peebles and his puritanical outlook.

It even came to a point one day where Ernest, a strapping young man six feet tall, offered to fight Johnny Caruthers. I stepped in: "You'll have to fight me first, before you'll hit a seventy-year-old man," I told him. Ernest backed down. But Johnny Caruthers was ready, more than ready, to duke it out with him.

It was some time later, after I'd quit the job, that I visited Johnny Caruthers in the hospital. He was very diminished, not at all the cocky and obstinate man I'd known during our working days, and I felt contrite that I'd treated him so shabbily. He died the next day.

During this period I was ensconced at the Palmore, 519 Prospect Street, in the hill district of El Paso, only a few blocks from Roscoe's digs, a tiny but very comfortable room with a balcony which looked out over the gold-ore glitter of Juárez. I was embroiled now in a reconstruction of the failed novel I'd churned out some months earlier in LA, a book based on the many letters I'd written for the beautiful butterflies of Mariscal Street. I didn't know exactly what I was trying to accomplish, but it had somehow to do with the hundreds of lives I'd touched, however peripherally, in writing the letters for the girls. There were soldiers and sailors out there, and *braceros* and truck drivers, and steel workers and traveling salesmen, Germans, Russians, Spaniards, Italians, Poles, Arabs, Swedes, Tuniseans, Tongans, Fiji Islanders and Frenchmen, and I knew their histories. All of these men— and the women... In each a microcosm, in each a story, in each a life. The books which the world favors proffer as the hero a politician, a general, a CEO, a movie director or a homicide detective. *But what about the rest of us?* I believe that the life of the commonest man or woman—the janitor, the waitress, the mechanic, the telephone operator, the truck driver, the prostitute, the barmaid—is worth recounting, if it's presented with verve and style and panache. In our hearts we're all princes and potentates, queens and prima ballerinas. Our failure to achieve our aims may be attributed to human weakness, but the dream remains. And what is literature, if not the realm where fantasy and reality converge? Open your beaks, my little songbirds, and spill it out—your dreams, your frustration, your disappointment, your rage, your reconciliation. The scope of the work that I was trying to bring into being was impossibly and ridiculously vast. It encompassed innumerable lives, dreams, and destinies. It was an attempt to get at the germ of humanity that glows in each tiny heart, in the heart of the common soldier, the bricklayer, the carpenter, the busboy, the taxi driver, the elevator operator. The rank and file, their crazy dreams, their abysmal horizons, their pathetic hopes, their terrifying courage, their hearts laid bare, what they loved, what they hated, what they feared, what they believed.

I gave it my best, I gave it everything, but I couldn't begin to pull it together. I'd reached too far. I'd tried to throw a lasso loop around the whole world. I knew I was wrong but I couldn't give up. Misgivings multiplied in my mind like shrieking banshees. Maybe I wasn't a writer after all. Maybe I'd be better off doing something else. What about selling real estate? Or Christmas supplies? Or ballpoint pens? It was a crazy enterprise, one that was doomed from the start by virtue of its overweening ambition. What I had envisioned was nothing less than an intimate and in-depth portrait of every man and woman on earth—*The Autobiography of Everybody.*

12

WITH A PORTION of his Beneficial Finance loot Roscoe bought a car, a beat-up old Dodge, and one weekend just before the car completely collapsed we drove over to the town of Quick Draw, near Las Cruces, to visit Roscoe's Uncle Luther. It promised to be a peaceful interlude, so I brought along a favorite book, *The Maze and the Minotaur* by John Calvin Ryder, and Roscoe brought his bible, *The Decay of the Angel* by Yukio Mishima. And, of course, his folded newspaper, his *carte d'identité*.

There was nothing much to Quick Draw except a boarded-up gas station with a battered red Coke machine, a sign, "Welcome to Quick Draw, pop. 174," and open country and more open country. We turned right at a dirt road past the gas station and pulled up at a lonely prairie house that perched uneasily on the hardpan like a marooned ship. The slowly spinning blades of a windmill crowned a privy, a bunkhouse and the wreck of a barn. A rheumy-eyed cow dog trotted out to meet us, barking his head off.

"Quick Draw! We made it." Roscoe proclaimed. "Don't worry about Shep. He won't bother you. Come on, let's get some breakfast."

We went inside and I met Uncle Luther, a silver haired

cowboy. His skin, baked by the relentless desert sun, was wrinkled like old shoe leather. But it was cozy in there, and a tiny electric fan offered some relief from the heat.

The kitchen was filled with heavenly cooking smells. We sat down at the wobbly plastic table and Luther dished up bacon, eggs and home fries. While Roscoe and I were stuffing our faces, Uncle Luther stood at the stove, stirring a chili pot with a big spoon. He tasted the chili, and then offered a spoonful to the dog.

"What d'you think, Shep? Needs comino?" He turned to face us, waving the spoon. "Say, can you boys stay for a few days?"

I was hoping Roscoe would say yes, not just for my sake, but for Uncle Luther's sake. It must have been a lonely life for the old man with nobody for company but that droopy-eyed cow dog and the occasional Gila monster.

"Thanks, Uncle Luther, but we gotta be getting back..."

It was true. This was long after Roscoe had been fired from Sears, but he'd recently picked up a job busing tables in a cafeteria. He and the little woman were back in the apartment on Prospect Street and Roscoe was once again trying halfheartedly to go straight.

"That's too bad. I'm makin' chili."

"Whoops! Well, that's different, Uncle Luther. We'll stick around!"

Luther sat down at the table with his plate. He fed the dog a piece of bacon.

"Good chili takes time. And you don't put beans in chili. Did you know that, boy?"

"No, I didn't, Uncle Luther."

"You don't put tomaters, neither."

After breakfast we went out to take a look at the site of the old Curly Wolf Saloon, later called the Quick Draw Saloon, where Texas badman John Wesley Hardin shot and killed a half Indian gunslinger named Cherokee George in 1869, but there was nothing to see except a weathered wooden marker.

Roscoe and I slept that night in the bunkhouse, like regular ranch hands. The stillness was monumental. When I finally woke up it was afternoon. Luther, in the kitchen, was stirring his big pot of chili. Roscoe, sprawled on the couch, was drinking a beer, reading Mishima and watching a nature special on TV. Shep was snoozing on the floor. On the screen, tarantulas were mating. Their cautious furry-limbed sparring reminded me of Ysela and the boxer, and I wondered if they were not doing the same thing at that very moment.

There was no running water at Uncle Luther's. The water came up from the ground. You had to pump it at an old-time pump out by the bunkhouse. That water tasted like sulfur but it was perfectly okay to drink, Uncle Luther assured us. But we didn't concern ourselves all that much with water because the fridge was crammed full of Pabst Blue Ribbon beer, and more cases were stacked in the pantry.

Uncle Luther's chili was worth the wait. Smoking hot cornbread poked full of butter rounded out the meal, and we washed everything down with plenty of PBR.

I don't know how many days we stayed in Quick Draw. It wasn't long. Roscoe got somebody to take his shift at the cafeteria and everything was cool, but he was itching now to get back to Mariscal Street. Why had we come in the first place, I'd begun to wonder? Just to touch bases, I figured. Roscoe needed to prove to himself that he still belonged somewhere in the world, in the American world. He could have stayed on in Quick Draw, we both could have. Uncle Luther assured us of that repeatedly. And do what? Subsistence farming? I suppose we could have carried it off. Luther had a few rows of beans and tomatoes, plus a flock of feeble-minded chickens that pecked everywhere in the dust. But it was a poor option. The emptiness of Quick Draw would have throttled the life out of us. The nearest town of any size was Las

Cruces, a hundred miles distant. You could go into the town of Quick Draw, of course, but the town of Quick Draw consisted of nothing but that ruin of a gas station, the battered red Coke machine, the lonesome wooden Cherokee George marker, and the sign, "Welcome to Quick Draw, pop. 174." And where were the other hundred and seventy-three residents of Quick Draw, might a person ask? In the bone orchard, I imagine, or maybe the desert had swallowed them up.

One night we heard something like the trumpeting of a bull elk being strangled by a boa constrictor. It was the old man baying at the moon. It was a regular thing, I learned. "The moon," Roscoe informed me. "The full moon sends him clean off his nut." Then there were the nightmares. You could hear him shouting all the way out in the bunkhouse. Every night he was wrestling with ghosts, most likely the phantom crew of his shipwrecked prairie home. I even imagined I could see Uncle Luther, that sun-baked iguana of a man, walking around outside the house in his nightshirt, tugging at the rigging and muttering, "Needs comino, Shep. Yep, needs comino."

Good Christ! I was getting as antsy as Roscoe.

One morning while I was in the kitchen eating breakfast—Luther was making chili once again—Roscoe got up and went outside, with Shep at his heels. Through the kitchen window I could see him walking with a staggering gait. He wandered out on the empty prairie and flung his arms to the sky. The stillness was getting to him, I could tell. He couldn't take it. Roscoe needed confusion and trouble in his life. It was time to go back to Mexico. Luther gave me a hopeless look, then stepped to the kitchen window and stood gazing out at Roscoe and Shep. After a moment he returned to the stove and tasted the chili with his big spoon.

"Needs comino," he said sadly. "Yep, needs comino."

13

A FRIDAY IN SEPTEMBER and I'm invited to Roscoe's digs on Prospect for dinner, to be followed by a trip to an uncle's place in the sticks thirty miles south of Ciudad Juárez. They're having fried Spam, which is fine with me. Food is food, and food is good, period. Pilar doesn't seem any too glad to see me, which doesn't come as a surprise.

We gulp down our rations, huddled at the spindly kitchen table like a family of field mice in the half darkness with the TV going in the other room. Fried Spam, Tiptop Bread, refried beans, Oreo Cookies, and to wash it down, weak warm cherry Koolaid in plastic glasses. *Bebé* Linda is asleep on the floor with her *chupón* in her mouth, and Monalisa's in the bedroom, asleep under the framed photograph of Dostoevsky that Roscoe has mounted on the wall over his bed. I find it strange to think of Monalisa sleeping in a real bed instead of on her pile of rags on the dirt floor of the mud hut on *Calle O* in Colonia Alta Vista.

After the meal, while Pilar sullenly scrapes the plates, Roscoe digs in the refrigerator and comes up with a bottle of Urdiñola. We sit in the living room, on the couch, staring at the TV. After a moment I get up and turn off the sound. That way I can stand it. Roscoe cracks the bottle open, takes a swig and puts on a record, Javier Solis,

"*Sombras Nada Mas.*" He belches and hands me the bottle. He's pissed off about his domestic situation and he's got to get it out.

"They're completely mercenary, these women! Whores every one of them! She wanted a refrigerator and I got it for her, then she wanted a Waring blender and I got her that, and now by Christ she wants a fucking toaster oven. And all this just to get her to open her legs for five minutes. I mean, what's the big deal? You'd think she had the fucking Taj Mahal between her legs…"

I'm going to tell you about one of Roscoe's quirks. Nearly every day—in the earlier days, I mean, before he lost the Sears job—he'd skip out of work at the Sears keys and engraving counter, defiantly extending his lunch break. He'd march home, a matter of a few blocks, forcibly clear everybody out, Pilar and *Bebé* Linda, pull the curtains and turn on the TV and shuck off his clothes—all but the shoes and socks—and jerk off to "American Bandstand." This was Roscoe's daily treat, the climax of his existence, his little joypop. He even sprayed Pilar's perfume around the room to make it seem more real. But now that Monalisa's staying with them, Roscoe bitterly complains— sick, languishing in the bedroom, or lying on her army cot in the kitchen—it's impossible.

"A man doesn't like to jack off in front of his mother-in-law," he declares grimly, choking down a furious gulp of Urdiñola.

Pilar grudgingly serves *café* and we discuss the trip to the country. Pilar, derisively pretending that she doesn't know that I understand, tells Roscoe in Spanish that under no circumstances am I to go with them. When she condescends to look at me, malice gleams in her eyes like thrown hatchets.

"If there's going to be a problem…" I venture in English, gazing in mock-seriousness at Roscoe.

"Just leave everything to me," Roscoe tosses back nonchalantly, sweetening his coffee with a shot of

Urdiñola.

Fifteen minutes later the conversation has degenerated into a drunken argument between Pilar and Roscoe as to whether Roscoe and I will go over to Mariscal Street and hit a few of the cantinas and meet Pilar later at the Bottle Club, where I'm to pick up Ysela, my date for the weekend, or whether we should all three go directly to the Bottle Club and then out to the uncle's place in the country. In the midst of the squabble, just as it's getting to the biting and clawing stage, Pilar marches out to a pay phone and calls a taxi. That was Pilar's answer to everything: call a taxi. She was defiantly extravagant with money, one of the few things I admired about her. It was a good thirty miles to Colonia La Cuesta and we could just as well have taken a bus. To see Pilar piss away the money, out of spite, even though her family might be hungry the next day, filled me with a new respect for her.

At the Bottle Club we paused just long enough to pick up Ysela, then we piled back into the taxi. We'd be going to a dance at the Hipodromo after the visit with the uncle, Pilar informed us. There were five of us, Roscoe and Pilar in the front seat, and Ysela and me in the back—and Rosana, a buddy of Pilar's from the early days when she, Pilar, answered to the name Olga, her whoring name, and sat in booths in the Navy Rose Club, stiffly dispensing affection to soldiers and truck drivers who handled her familiarly and bought her fifty-cent *copas*.

Before the dance at the Hipodromo, we spent a few hours at the house of Jesús Ramos, Pilar's uncle, in Colonia La Cuesta, thirty miles south of Ciudad Juárez on the road to Casas Grandes. A hut, like a Navajo hogan, looked out on a vegetable garden and a rusted-out car squatting on wooden blocks. Other wreckage of machinery surrounded the hut, decapitated engine blocks, rusty transmissions, tangles of ancient exhaust pipes, powdered windshields, piles of old tires and a gutted washing machine. A few chickens and pigs poked around in the debris, and a fluffy smiling burro was tethered to the front bumper of the wrecked car.

Jesús's wife Mercedes was a woman who, by all appearances, had attained the very pinnacle of success. She beamed and curtsied, hitching up her skirts as she served *café*. She scraped the plates, boiled a kettle of rice, brushed the children's hair and swept the dirt floor of the hut, then slopped the pigs and shooed the chickens, all with the Cinderella air of a fairy princess who has inherited a magic kingdom. She radiated a simple happiness and a buoyant delight in being alive. In her spare moments, after bustling feather-light around the room, tidying everything up, she sat gazing into a jagged fragment of mirror glass taped to the adobe wall, exactly like Felisa's mirror, brushing out her long hair with a dreamy expression on her face, a Polynesian-orgasm look of rapturous softness and bliss. Her face, very primitive, with arched eyebrows, thickly lidded eyes and thick oily lips, glistened with minuscule beads of sweat. I adored her immediately. The folds under the eyes, which were somehow devastatingly attractive, accentuated the eyes themselves, their expression of somnolent heaviness, stoicism combined with a fatalistic lascivious gleam. This was a woman who worshipped life with her being, and her being was a flame.

Jesús Ramos himself was an *Indio* who looked like an Aztec god. There were only a few facets to his character, but these facets were drawn with a crude black line on an uncluttered canvas: pride, strength and simplicity. Jesús Ramos wasn't trying to *understand* life; he was living it— with courage, with gusto, with dignity. He liked his meals and he liked his bottle of drink. Women, he handled tenderly, like children and animals. What an excellent man he was, a real hombre. He was certain of his place in the world's hierarchy. Christ, what I wouldn't have given to trade places with him! I felt like a shadow beside the man. Yet he treated me as though I were his equal, a *compadre*, like I was one of Villa's soldiers; no, like I was Pancho

Villa himself.

In the dirt yard, flanked by piles of junk, we passed a fuming bottle of tequila back and forth, Jesús Ramos and me. He clapped me on the back, and then we Indian wrestled, a little friendly horseplay while we waited for the girls to put on their makeup. At the same time he was shrewdly taking measure of me. Jesús Ramos was a foot shorter than me and bowlegged, in a white shirt, with very dark skin, a ferocious Viva Zapata mustache and a dangerous gleam in his eye. Shoving the bottle at me, he told me gravely in Spanish how he'd killed a man three years ago in a fair fight. Lurching suddenly around, flinging his arm toward the mountain peaks directly south, he pointed to a grave fifty feet away in the sagebrush. We ambled a few steps into the desert, stopping to palaver, and pretty soon we came upon a white wooden cross. Jesús Ramos had given his enemy a decent burial.

"He is undoubtedly a skeleton by now," Jesús Ramos said as we both stared at the grave, me with the bottle of tequila in my paw.

"Undoubtedly."

There are so many graves in Mexico!

The dance at the Hipodromo was a roller derby, a joyous sweating stomp. The Mexican polka was the thing, with a ragged heroic orchestra belting it out. There were two floors to the place, a balcony overlooking the tables and dance floor—a circular track—and downstairs the bar. We commandeered a table, ordered drinks and plunged into the fray, Ysela and I, Roscoe and Pilar, and Jesús Ramos and some honey he immediately picked up (Mercedes had remained behind with the chickens, and somehow we lost Rosana before we even sat down).

Around and around we went. It's beautiful once you get your feet wet. We were all welded together by centrifugal force. As the circle of dancers jammed past the tables, everybody grabbed bottles and swallowed enormous gulps of *cerveza* and tequila.

The musicians wore tight-fitting uniforms and dusty black shoes. They had walked across plowed fields and vacant lots choked with weeds and junk to get to the Hipodromo from their huts in the bush, lugging their instrument cases. They stood up to their instruments like gladiators. They worked like carpenters or brick masons, intent, sincere, giving it everything, from the heart. They were artisans who loved their work; they lived for it and by it. Each time Ysela and I hurtled past the bandstand I saw the young drummer sweating in a sparkly black shirt open at the throat, his hopeful haircurl cascading down over a feverish pinched face.

Around and around, feet stomping the boards—it's an athletic contest, this desperate exuberance. When a couple falls down, others rush joyously to trample them, or purposely trip over their bodies and sprawl in a delighted heap. It's a celebration of the body, communion at the herd level, the thighs pumping, bone and muscle straining, the arms flailing, the blood singing in the veins, the head reeling. A paroxysm of froth and sweat, everybody wedged in, flirtations of all sorts, frantic guzzling, near fist fights, this flesh-consummation charged with raw Roman splendor and pagan enthusiasm. Around and around we went, faster and faster—the Wheel of Life and Death, tigers chasing their tails and melting down into butter. Beautiful golden butter.

When we left the Hipodromo, Jesús Ramos fell down in the street and two cops came walking up to haul him in. I was just getting into the taxi with Ysela and the others. Drunk as I was, I hopped out of the taxi and rescued him, right under the nose of the fuzz. I delivered an authoritative speech in Spanish that left those shit-lovers nonplused and teetering like two birds perched on a clothesline. I packed Jesús Ramos into the cab and got in. I put my arm around Ysela. She barfed and passed out, sagging against my chest. I felt great.

"*Andale, pues,*" I ordered the driver. "*Vámanos!*"

Once we were underway, I slapped Jesús Ramos's face, rousing him long enough for him to dictate his address deliriously to the speeding driver who jammed through stop signs and took the most amazing chances with utter fatalistic calm. He was ready to die for a trifle. We all were.

And so we took our drunken Jesús home...

14

DOYCE COTTON was one of Roscoe's boyhood chums from Charleston who had become a "success." He traveled for a pharmaceutical company. Doyce, Roscoe informed me at the Rosita Club where we met for a drink early on an overcast Friday afternoon, was stopping by El Paso on business and wanted to hit Juárez and do the town. So it was to be the grand tour with all the trimmings. We were to meet Doyce in El Paso, at "Alligator Park"—San Jacinto Plaza—in the center of town, that very night. It was all arranged. And tonight was a special night in Ciudad Juárez, Roscoe reminded me. It was soldiers' payday night, and the red-light quarter would be jumping.

Roscoe had the idea of trying for a loan, a big loan. But there was a drawback. The man, according to Roscoe, was unbelievably tight with his loot. The evening, therefore, Roscoe explained, would be a program engineered to soften Doyce up for the precise moment when Roscoe would pop the question. Which meant that, to begin with, we'd have to buy our own drinks, which also meant, since we were both broke, that we'd have to stop by the Navy Rose to borrow a few dollars from Angel Mike before meeting Doyce at Alligator Park.

Roscoe was wearing a white shirt and a tie, I noticed. And he'd shined his shoes. With his folded newspaper, his *carte d'identité*, and that serious expression on his mug he could almost have passed as a regular citizen.

"And don't go hitting him up for dimes and quarters, okay?" he cautioned in a tone bordering on hysteria as we headed for the Navy Rose. "Don't get pissed off. You know how you are. This loan means a lot to me. It means my marriage. It means my life."

And on and on he yammered, like a subway desperado plotting to knock over a gumball machine. But as it turned out we didn't get the money from Angel Mike, because Angel Mike didn't come to work that evening; consequently we began sponging drinks off Doyce immediately after meeting him at Alligator Park and crossing back over to Juárez on the *tranvia*, thus alienating him rather early in the evening, or at least I did. And Roscoe confronted Doyce and delivered his hard-luck story not at the propitious moment as he'd carefully planned and rehearsed, but drunkenly across the table at Irma's Club at three in the morning in a hateful manner full of scorn and contempt, the contempt which Roscoe expressed so easily, a speech which numbed Doyce...

I don't know how to describe Doyce Cotton. I won't try. But he looked as if he'd been on a coffee jag. I could see right off the bat that he disapproved of me. He was clearly shocked to see Roscoe in such a state, and his scornful glances told me that he considered me responsible. The whole affair seemed so ludicrous to me that it was all I could do to keep from laughing in his face. I sensed that Roscoe would have rough sledding with Doyce, and the evening bore me out.

On the *tranvia*, Doyce repeatedly questioned Roscoe about the girls. Apparently, he hadn't been with a woman in months. Roscoe answered in his usual bantering way, keeping up a stream of flashy talk, glancing at me for approval, slipping in lightning bursts of Spanish, quick double entendres, parenthetically mimicking Doyce, dancing around him like a shaman weaving a spell.

The first place we hit, because Doyce insisted, was the Follies, a tourist-class strip joint on Avenida Juárez, the main drag. I'd never been to the Follies before. It was hardly the sort of place I would have gone to of my own free will. We sat at a table draped with a gravy-stained white tablecloth. The girl in the spotlight was naked as a goldfish but somehow utterly sexless and unappealing. She stood there snapping her gum and grinding her pelvis in a bored, half-hearted way, as though she were fiercely dedicated to making everything seem commonplace and banal. And the beery orchestra with its farting trombones! *Such world-weariness...* "We are all victims," some author once said, and I never felt the truth of his statement like I felt it at that moment sitting in the Follies watching that bored *señorita* plodding drearily through her bumps and grinds, while at the white-draped tables the sweating American tourist women sat with their souvenir glasses and ceramic donkeys, and the half-sodden husbands with their sappy smiles and flowered shirts and their arms full of glittery junk. It made me want to cry. *Betrayed! For this we descended from the trees! Why wouldn't we be just as well off to live in the open and hunt rabbits with a stick?*

But at the same time there was an air about the place of sappy, chowder-headed bliss that made me think back to functions I attended as a child, a fireman's picnic, for example, and a wheezy, farting orchestra tuning up on an afternoon at a lake somewhere, the softball game just getting underway, the hotdogs sizzling, the beer cans being popped open, or a keg being tapped, and the air blue with wood smoke, and everyone half in the bag and splashing around in the water—the sun-kissed children, the sneezing, cow-like women, and the stubble-bearded trombone man sweating in his undershirt in the sun—the indescribable feeling of small-town America on a Sunday afternoon, which, moony and moronic as it may be, is nevertheless in my blood.

Looking back was a luxury I rarely permitted myself. But after this initial visit to the Follies with Doyce, I began hitting the place regularly, usually early in the evening, to get sloshed before assaulting Mariscal Street. Always, when I dropped by the Follies, the effect was the same. A sappy, boozy, nostalgic feeling engulfed me. I had a few drinks and I shed a few tears. I loved colliding with the jolly, brittle world of Mariscal Street when I was in a dewy, sentimental mood. It lent a surreal quality to the evening. All in all, I'm glad I made that stop with Doyce. From that night forward, whenever I felt like having a good cry, I simply dropped into the Follies and watched the girls take it off.

As we passed in front of the Palacio de Oro, Roscoe suddenly whipped off his tie—*my tie* that I'd loaned him earlier in the week. He handed it to a street musician he'd been gabbing with.

"Hey! How come you gave that joker my tie?"

"Because he asked me for it."

We ducked into a bar. A brightly-painted whore was taunting a fat man, playfully spanking his enormous belly. "*Estás embarazado?*" she shrilled mockingly. "Eh? Are you pregnant? *Digame, pues. Estás embarazado? No tenga verguenza, cochino marrano!*" The fat man lurched drunkenly, knocking over tables and chairs and smashing bottles and glasses. As we strolled out, the girl was choked with laughter.

Soldiers' payday night in Juárez was a cyclical celebration comparable to the spring solstice, except in Juárez this pagan festival occurred once a month instead of annually. The way the red-light quarter blossomed was phenomenal. It was a rebirth, a re-generation, a primordial resurgence of the life force, an affirmation of life and of sexuality. Above all, it was a joyous re-entrenchment of "business as usual."

As we approached the Cairo Club a girl called to me from a doorway: "*Oyes, pescado...*"

Pescado, that's what the girls say. That's what they call us—fish, suckers, marks—*pescados*. *Pescado*, yep, that's me—*Americano, gabacho, guero, pinche Inglés*—*pescado*. I'm the finnan haddie and the lox and bagels and the pickled herring all rolled into one, the Nordic adventurer swimming in anchovy paste. That's how they see us devils from *el norte* when we're packed sardine-tight into their bars on soldiers' payday night; that's how we appear in their eyes. We're the blond-beasts, the big bloodthirsty bastards with the fat wallets and the big pointed dicks and tight scrotums loaded with the ice-cold sperm of demons.

I often thought about that, I wondered about it, I envisioned it, how they thought of us *pescados*, how they pictured us, I mean, when things were slack, in the lean days each month leading up to soldiers' payday. During those slack days before soldiers' payday, Mariscal Street was utterly lifeless. In every cantina it was the same. The girls huddled around the *calientón* listlessly painting their nails, reading *Doctor Corazón*, knitting baby things. Mariachis tossed pennies with street boys. Pushcart vendors subsisted on their own wares. The tiny *loncherías* were empty. The cash register was silent. They probably pictured us, the girls, during those lean days, piled up in cold storage, frozen solid, goggle-eyed, with gaping mouths and stiff, useless fins, stacked in the barracks, up to the ceiling, a layer of fish, a layer of ice, a layer of fish and a layer of ice. *Pescados*.

Then comes the Day, the thrice-hallowed Day when the eagle drops his guano and we all emerge from cold storage in a great influx, *Americanos, gabachos, pescados*, wiggling our tails like salmon, frantically forging upstream, loaded with money and sperm. Here we come—the bloated sausages from the hinterlands, the *brattwurst*, the *braunschweiger*, the blood-sausage and the bonefish and the *polska kielbase*, the beef-trust, the beef-injection crew. Mariscal Street, on soldiers' payday night, is a meat market, a *carnicería*, a flesh auction, a butcher's bench. Just hoist your sex up on the scales. Hokay, Johnny! You no come, you no pay nothing. Whack! Forty *centavos!* A pound of flesh! You likey dance, Johnny? Hokay, Johnny! Cheep price! *No pagas mucho*, Johnny! Short time! Chopped meat! Five dolla! *Inspección!* Skin it back! A dime for the music! *Bailamos?* You weesh to buy hot books? Hurry up, Johnny. You no come pretty soon, Johnny?

Come. That's the word for tonight: *come.* Tonight a white frothy river is welling up behind the sperm-drunk eyes of the girls, behind their sated Giaconda smiles. A tidal wave of sperm is surging through the streets of Juárez, foaming in the gutters, flooding the cantinas, wrenching roofs off houses, floating the joists, fertilizing everything. Tonight Mother Juárez is a woman with a million oviducts, a flesh-city suffused with the orgasmic glow of mob estrus. Rolling her magical eyes, blowing luminous bubbles of sperm, she clutches at madly spurting genitals, pressing them against her udders, against the lush female sprawl of her cityscape. She tenders the hot milky streams like a harbormaster, joyfully marshaling them between her great fellaheen thighs. Tonight Mother Juárez is a Jezabel with the taste of spunk in her mouth and the feel of money in her pocket. Tonight the womb is opened. Tonight poets and warriors are conceived; statesmen and murderers are engendered. Tonight bread rises, milk clabbers, orchards bloom. Tonight there is music in the streets. The cash register is jingling again.

We ducked into to the Blue Fox—El Zorro Azul. Already things were beginning to fizzle because Doyce had only one thing on his mind, the girls, and we wanted to drink, Roscoe and I. Already, as anyone might have predicted, Doyce resented having to spring for all the drinks, plus Roscoe had the nerve, right there on the sidewalk, while we were on our way to the Blue Fox, to hit Doyce up for the price of a pint of Urdiñola. Roscoe was afraid now that the evening would be cut short because once Doyce got his nuts off, he'd be heading for the barn in order to save money.

In the toilet at the Blue Fox, by a stroke of luck, I ran into Arturo, a flower vendor I knew from innumerable nights in the bars. He was snoozing standing up at the urinal. He looked like an idol with the gold leaf peeled off, the naked clay of his face frozen in a sardonic grin as he stared down at the white petals of his wilted begonias floating in the trough. He reminded me of the Aztec rain god Xochipilli, the Flower Prince.

After an exchange of pleasantries, I asked Xochipilli the all-important question: "Can you lend me five bucks American?"

The Blue Fox, where I'd often been a patron, featured a plush, dark interior, so dark you couldn't tell what was going on, which in a good many instances was all for the best. The philosophy of attack was that the girls insisted on dancing. They voraciously dragged one to the floor. They relied on body contact plus a lot of fast throaty talk delivered close to the ear while dancing pelvis to pelvis. The prices were high, five and six dollars, and the *copas* were a buck fifty. All the girls wore evening dresses. And there were white tablecloths on the tables. They maintained a certain standard at the Blue Fox. There was no *calientón*, and unlike the crummier, more comfortable dives, they didn't permit sleeping in the booths.

After drinks all around, with Doyce reluctantly shelling out, Roscoe set Doyce up with Concha, "*La Chichona*" (big tits), as we called her, a very exciting woman, always a crisp satin gown, never drunk or maudlin like so many whores, but cool, soft-spoken and rather distant. Concha and I had approached the point of copulating on only one occasion. We discussed the price, seven bucks, which I didn't have, and it was admittedly high, the going rate on Mariscal Street being four dollars, but I was terribly intrigued by the brisk, businesslike way she offered herself, just take it or leave it, as though she were mentioning the price of an article of furniture, a bookcase or an armchair. I spent several evenings with Concha, buying *copas* and dancing, but she never permitted me to take liberties. That intrigued me too. A fascinating woman, Concha.

Anyway, Concha was *La Reina*, the absolute queen of the lot, and Roscoe and I did Doyce a real favor in presenting him to her. I'm almost certain she would have been compassionate with him. But characteristically, Doyce balked at the price. I was almost glad. It seemed easier now that we were going to fleece him, or rather that Roscoe was. I never believed in the success of Roscoe's plan, nor did I have any interest in it. Roscoe kept mentioning some insane figure like five hundred dollars. I assured him that all I wanted to do was get drunk.

Next stop, the Navy Rose, where Roscoe endeavored to set Doyce up with Sandra. But, as I might have predicted, this second date we procured for Doyce commenced to fizzle also. Sandra got into one of her moods. She was pissed off at Roscoe for bringing Doyce to her and thus "treating her like a whore," a posture which I found ridiculous. As we sat together in the booth, the four of us, she began slinging them down. I could feel the violence and tears rising up in her.

It was laughable, all the same. "*Estamas en las camas?*" This was how Doyce tried to express, "Do you want to go to bed with me?" Sandra punched him in the belly, playfully, yes, but with enough force to knock the wind out of him. Sandra thought nothing of socking a fellow, of beating the hell out of him in fact, all with a jolly smile and an enticing purr of bedroom talk. It was her little girl's way of getting even. Doyce sat by, dumbfounded, with his arm awkwardly draped around Sandra's shoulders, trying in his agonized way to feel one of her *chiches*. She dug her sharp little fingernails into his arm and scratched him in that playful, seemingly innocent way of hers that contained a good deal of careless puppy-like malice, or careless kittenish malice. She attacked him with cruel violence, humorously exaggerated for my benefit and for Roscoe's.

"Cheepis-*skate!* Where is your *mather?* Son of a bitch. You want to feel my *chiches?*" This, with a few haughty looks down her flared nostrils at Roscoe, scornful but sexily inviting. To me she was friendly, tauntingly so. I basked in the warmth of her gaze, which seemed to ask, "Why do you hang around with such trash?"

Because I felt sorry for Doyce, dumbly bearing the brunt of Sandra's attack, I turned her attention to Roscoe by pointing out the scratches Pilar had engraved on his face and hands during one of their recent knockdown-dragouts. But my ploy backfired. Sandra lit into Roscoe, reopening their old wound. "Why do you bring me such a pig as this?" she demanded in Spanish. "Is this one of your countrymen? *Pfui!* You *guero* son of a bitch! Where is your wife, the *puta* you married? You have no respect. *Tienes obligación!* Why do you not earn money for your *bebés?* Eh? All your money, you spend on fucking. You think only of your peter. *Malcriado!*" She ripped her red crinoline dress down the middle, baring her breasts, and yelled at Doyce, "Hey! You want my *chiches? Puto! Maricón! Toma!* Take it! Eat it! *Gabacho* son of a bitch! Hey, *you!*"

Just at this moment the bartender—a new man, he'd only been at the Rose for a few weeks—came shuffling out from behind the bar, hesitantly brandishing a varnished wooden billy club. He was a sedate individual, middle-aged, a fussbudget who would have been more at home selling gardening supplies than tending bar in a whorehouse. Chewing his words through his mustache, he threatened to call the *federales.* His sense of propriety was wounded, and all because of Sandra's little *chiches*, her tiny bare breasts, which were nothing to write home about anyway. It made me laugh. So Sandra stormed off to her room after scratching Doyce and frightening him half to death and roundly cursing us all: "*Putos, cabrónes, marijuanos!*"

"I've got it," Roscoe exclaimed as we hit the street. "The Luz de Luna! Minga!"

"Sure," I murmured. "The Peruvian Pelvis…"

"Who? What? What did you say? The Peruvian Pelvis?" Doyce sputtered. He was beside himself.

We hotfooted it to the Luz de Luna, but Minga wasn't on duty that night, so we hit the Green Lantern, the Durango Club, the Delicias, the Adelita and the Foreign Club. And more. But in every case, either the price was too high or the girl wasn't quite ravishing enough. As we stood at the urinal in the Tango Club, Roscoe and I, Roscoe suggested that we simply bop Doyce over the head and take his poke. I laughed in Roscoe's face. But he was serious. He was frantic. His one fixed idea was that he would get the money. I felt mellow.

"Look, we're having a good time, aren't we?" I ventured. "Why not let it go at that?"

So we went to El Lago Blanco, another white-tablecloth joint. The girls were polite, as though it were a church supper. It was there at El Lago Blanco, the White Lake Club, that Roscoe, several months before, got us into a scrape with the *federales* because of a crazy obsession he had with the "Pecker Checker," a sprightly silver-haired lady whose station was in the hallway just behind the scarred wooden door that led to the girls' rooms. A standard feature in all of the fancier dives, the Pecker Checker was typically a woman of advanced years dressed in a nurse's rig whose function it was to inspect the dicks of the whores' customers before they went to the room. Following the *inspección*, one was expected to leave the lady a small tip, usually a quarter.

Roscoe insisted that this particular lady at the White Lake Club, when she examined his penis, took an inordinately long time in going about her business, that she was in fact "caressing it," as Roscoe put it. He actually went back several times, going to the room with any girl who happened to be available, for the express purpose of gaining an interview with the Pecker Checker, whose touch had become ecstasy to him due to the intensity of his obsession with her. I won't go into all of the details, but there were, for example, the interminable deliberations: was she caressing it or wasn't she? One night Roscoe decided to end the suspense. Midway through the examination he made a grab for her. She yelled bloody murder and the bartender immediately called the cops. We ducked into the street but were nabbed by two *federales*. We got off by emptying our pockets.

After the White Lake we allowed ourselves at Doyce's insistence to fall into the clutches of a taxi driver who took us to Irma's Club, a locally famous tourist-class whorehouse off the beaten track. The girls wore white seersucker smocks, like nurses. Everything was spotlessly clean, the white tiled floors freshly mopped, the maids hurrying with folded towels. There was the smell of benzene, of glycerin soap, of Clorox, of various fungicides and fumigants, and the soothing gurgle of running water everywhere. I felt myself sinking into a state of pleasant anesthesia. The place reminded me of a sanitarium, a retreat where you go to take the cold-water cure.

Even before the drinks arrived I was converged on and whisked away by one of the sisters of mercy. She took me to the room to "talk it over," as they say. In the back, the decor was the same: a white, sanitized world. I felt giddy, as if I'd been sniffing helium. As we stood facing each other in the vibrating blue light of the room, I had the impression that she was going to give me an inoculation— or an enema. Or maybe ask me for a urine specimen. She looked a little bit like Elsa Lanchester in "The Bride of Frankenstein," alluring with pouted lips, yet stonily forbidding in a weird laboratory sort of way. While she mechanically recited her pat speech in English, I coldly ran my hands over her breasts and hips. A perverse sort of excitement seized me, an excitement that had somehow to do with the impersonal quality of the interview. This interlude, when one goes to the room to talk it over, a standard feature—like the Pecker Checker—in all the classier joints in Ciudad Juárez, very much resembled the act of putting coins in a parking meter, the idea being to cop as many feels as possible before the meter runs out.

Since I'd spent innumerable nights on Mariscal Street not only buying affection but when I was broke making the rounds of the "free-feel circuit," I was well-schooled in delaying tactics. In this instance I led off by pretending to speak only German, shouting at her, "*Was? Saght? Hein?*" I followed up by repeatedly interrupting her spiel with inane, perplexing, or nonsensical questions—anything to prolong the interlude. I wish I could convey the sense of cold, frenetic excitement. It was like assaulting a dress dummy in the hypersexual ward of a madhouse. It was a ballet in a wax museum. A banquet is what it was, a smorgasbord, an erotic brunch, and before she marched off, exasperated, I managed to enjoy everything—*the hors d'oeuvres, the soup of the day, the salad, the papas fritas, the salsa* fresca and even, so to speak, the dessert. Everything but the main course.

When I rejoined Roscoe in the booth he'd just finished reading Doyce off, the venomous speech I touched upon earlier, and Doyce had finally gone to the room with one of the love-dolls. Roscoe hurriedly downed Doyce's drink and scooped Doyce's change off the table with a theatrical flourish. He wanted to leave. I insisted that we wait for Doyce. A moment later Doyce came out, sweating and dazed. There had been a squabble between Doyce and one of the chambermaids. I went back to see what it was. By this time the bartender was back there also, inches from my face, brandishing his billy club. The beef, I discovered, was over a silver money clip. Doyce claimed that one of the girls had stolen it. I advised him to forget it. But he persisted. I was certain by now that someone had called the *federales*. I hurried out of the hallway that led to the *cuartos* and glanced across the room at Roscoe. He was on his feet. We scrammed out the side exit, abandoning Doyce to his fate.

After hitting the lopsided doorman at the Old West

Club up for a ten-spot, Roscoe and I dove into a tiny *lonchería* on *Calle Ugarte*. Food was now the primary thing. We sat at joint's single table while gaunt scavenger dogs limped past us like ghosts. Just as the eggs arrived, we were set upon by three grimy mariachis—"the Pudgy Musicians of Morning"—is the phrase that kept zinging though my head. A violin, a piccolo and a squeezebox accordion: an unusual combination, and they were an odd trio. They smelled money and they waded in relentlessly, like bloodsucking leeches, grimly serenading us. I ate as fast as I could with the deck lurching crazily and my stomach churning and the fiery grill spitting grease and fumes. The six of us—the three Musicians of Morning, Roscoe and me, and the cook—were squeezed like sardines into the toy-sized *lonchería* no bigger than a lobster trap. The saucer-eyed violinist with his soggy armpit hovered over my scrambled eggs and *chorizo*. I caught the gamy smell of the man's tattered clothing as he sawed away at the beat-up violin with heartrending sincerity. It was their *sincerity*, their utter *sincerity* that I couldn't get over.

After the meal we grabbed a bus. The passengers, most of them stolidly asleep, were survivors huddled in the wake of a disaster. We were soldiers returning from the front. The night had vomited up its leavings and we were it.

Immediately I fell asleep. I woke up with my head resting on a snorting *Indio's* shoulder and a white chicken was pecking at a banana peel near my foot. The rattletrap bus crammed with snoring bundles of rags jerked and roared through the dive-bombed streets. As we whipsawed around a blowhole, a *bracero* wrapped in a serape leaned over and threw up in the aisle. Already, I noticed, we were at the intersection of Avenida Cerveceria and Vicente Guerrero, way past our destination. It didn't seem to matter. I conked off again...

At Insurgentes a boy got on the bus with his guitar, leading his blind father who clutched a Styrofoam cup for catching coins. The boy belted out a song, "*Sin Sangre en*

Las Venas," gutbucket style, loud, brassy, courageous, with everyone asleep or completely uncaring.

Getting drunk had a sobering effect on me. I fell asleep and an instant later I woke up, my body electrified, my mind crystal clear, my bones vibrating like hollow icicles. That instant of sleep was like slipping on a banana peel, it was like stepping out for a breather between the acts; and when I woke up, as the boy got on the bus and began to sing, it was like stepping back in, and when I stepped back in everything was exactly the same as before except screwed up to twenty thousand decibels. The boy's gaudy courage electrified me, his flaming bravado. The music seemed to be pouring out of the blind man's rusty eyeholes. I felt pleasure and anguish too intense to endure. I glanced over at Roscoe. His mood was the same. We were now passing the Fraccionmento El Mirador, near the Colonia Palo Chino, miles beyond Colonia Alta Vista. No matter. There was a mutual desire, unspoken, to break the spell. The one thing I wanted now was to get off the bus, and after placing my feet gratefully on the green earth to lean fearlessly into a new day no matter how far I might be from my destination or what dangers I may face—but it must be *now*. I yank the cord. *I stop the bus*. Fingers of light are piercing my skull. The tour of the night is over. The stars are fading like scraps of rotten meat. A thin golden mist is drizzling down. Xochipilli is pissing on Ciudad Juárez.

15

ROSCOE VANISHED FOR A WHILE, dropped clean off the map. I went by all the usual haunts, the Rose, the Luz de Luna, the Rosita Club, the Old West, but no Roscoe. The midget doorman at the Durango Club was certain that Roscoe was in the chokey. The one-eyed old man with the street harp thought the same, and to emphasize the point he played a riff on his golden strings that seemed to say, "*Asi es la vida*." Paulo and Angel Mike concurred, but the doorman at the Old West said he'd seen Roscoe a month or so earlier getting into a taxi with a suitcase in his hand, and I began to think that he'd actually gone to Zihuatanejo and was at that very moment eating lobster under a thatched-roof palapa while a marimba band played on the shore. Or sitting in a skiff with a grizzled fisherman far out in Magdalena Bay where the great green sea turtles paddle to the surface, then sink slowly out of sight in the clear blue water. I even went by the Gusano Club. Josefina, behind the bar, was halfway congenial for a change. She hadn't seen Roscoe, either. "Good riddance," she added in Spanish under her breath as I sauntered out.

Then one day I ran into him, at the Hollywood Café of

all places. It turned out he'd spent a couple of months over in Quick Draw with Uncle Luther. What had he been doing in Quick Draw? Hiding from Pilar, of course, but…

"Well, I was…I was…trying to write." He seemed profoundly embarrassed.

"Write?" I exclaimed, grabbing his hand. "You mean a book? That's great, man! Really. I always thought you had it in you…"

Roscoe, obviously pleased, pumped my hand, but then went back to picking at his eggs and hemming and hawing.

"I always knew you were a writer," I continued. "I believe in you…"

"Yeah, well, I… Thanks, bro. I appreciate that. I tried. I cranked it out. I really did. But I couldn't get anything to jell. I mean it didn't seem to add up to anything. But I tried. I typed my ass off. I mean, I wrote literally thousands of pages. I thought… You know what I thought? I thought I was fucking Jack Kerouac."

"Maybe you were Jack Kerouac. You should have kept on with it."

On top of that, right about this time Ysela went back with Juan "El Indio" Mendoza. It was heartbreaking, but there was nothing I could do except return to my own corner and do a little quiet shadowboxing. I was outclassed, outranked. The guy was practically a national hero.

I tried seeing other women—Viridiana, at the Navy Rose Club, the "Six of Dominoes," Braulia at the Palacio de Oro, Concha "La Chichona" at the Blue Fox, even Minga, the Peruvian Pelvis, who, just as I'd suspected, was no more from Peru than I am. It cost me nearly a dozen *copas* to get it out of her, but she finally confessed that she hailed from a tiny Sonora town called Agua Prieta, which means, in Spanish, "Dirty Water."

I even went by the Catacombs, *Los Baños*. The faces of the women behind the iron bars had changed but the patter was the same: *"Hey Johnny! Suckie-fuckie? No pagas mucho. You no pay too much, Johnny!"*

It was no use trying to forget Ysela, I decided. I couldn't seem to fuck her off my mind. I was just another *pescado*, one more broken-hearted loser aimlessly wandering the Boulevard of Broken Dreams.

I was so downhearted that I didn't bother going to my job at the Chinese joint and just moped around all day. Roscoe was out of work too, and he was camping once again with the family in Colonia Alta Vista, but I knew if I went back there I'd lose face with Ysela entirely, so it happened that quite often I'd end up sleeping out with the coyotes. We even talked, Roscoe and I, about hitchhiking over to Quick Draw and throwing ourselves on Uncle Luther's tender mercies. I'm sure he would have taken us in.

Then, in January, Roscoe got on at a coffeehouse in El Paso called the Door, washing dishes and mopping up. The Door was a good place—that is, it was a building with walls, a roof and toilet facilities. What can I say? The winters are cold in Texas. I quickly wormed my way in, riding on Roscoe's coattails.

For several nights running, after a week had passed, Guy, the owner of the Door, trustingly assigned Roscoe to ring up pastries and coffee. These nights, until Guy got wise, we drank Charles Krug Fumé Blanc and ate blueberry muffins and baklava. As a business the coffeehouse was nowhere. Guy, an idealist, was trying frantically to keep it together. He hovered around the customers, fidgeting, smoking, chewing his nails, and talking, talking, talking. Roscoe was Guy's rococo saint, his little tin Jesus. Wherever Roscoe went, Guy was sure to follow, exactly like a puppy.

To Roscoe the world was one big mark, a duck to be popped off in a penny arcade. And yet Guy worshipped Roscoe like a god. He admired the *simplicity* of what he imagined to be Roscoe's stance. Simply, search, kill, eat, and stretch out in the sun. Then search and kill and eat again. When Guy saw Roscoe, he saw talons shredding fresh meat; he saw the hooked beak gulping it down. He saw Roscoe as an aboriginal man, a being totally governed by instinct, untouched by civilization, and I often thought how happy Roscoe might have been if only this were true, but unfortunately for Roscoe, he also had a mind. And Roscoe's mind was a cancer that had attached itself to a healthy animal, a cancer that, lamprey-like, was attempting to absorb its host by osmosis. This was the nature of Roscoe's struggle.

With me, Guy was very solicitous. He wanted to talk to me about Melville and Whitman, serious-like. I suppose I didn't give him a chance. But it reminded me too much of New York. What, exactly? Guy and Celeste, with their indoor complexions, the two of them, with their baggy sweaters and the constant smoking and their stale breath and the marijuana. And Morry, the hang-along who slithered behind them, a tiny peeled-shrimp of a man whose glazed cupcake face and perpetually watery-eyed expression made him look as if he'd just pulled himself off. There was even a creep who stumbled around muttering solemnly, "*One must imagine Sisyphus happy.*" The Door, with its ersatz New York underground atmosphere of crap and futility, represented to me everything I wanted to leave behind.

However, by remaining isolate I found the conditions very tolerable. Once it was established that I wanted to be left alone, I got on famously. What I wanted was a place to get in out of the weather—with bathroom privileges, of course—a cozy spot where I might curl up and read a book—and someone to bring me a sandwich now and then. No more than the average house pet might demand! I was deeply involved in a study of Dostoevsky during this period. I was rereading everything Dostoevsky wrote that was translated into English—and more important, from my standpoint, I was reading his letters—especially the letters he wrote from the prison in Siberia—and also I was reading every biography of Dostoevsky I could lay my hands on. *White Nights, Crime and Punishment, Dead Souls, A Raw Youth, The Possessed, The Lower Depths, The Brothers Karamazov*: these tomes I knocked back like so many shots of ice-cold vodka. What was burgeoning in my mind was Russia. Not the present-day Russia with its insipid religion of work founded by the bread-and-butter god, Karl Marx, the Jesus Christ of materialism, but the real Russia, the Russia that flourished when the tide of life ran high and the world was populated with real men and real women, God's Russia, Mother Russia, the Russia of white nights and humming samovars and fierce muzhiks and galloping troikas, the Russia of splendid, heroic women and cruel, passionate men, and floating high above it all, holy, banal, ridiculous, profound, honed by suffering to a luminous, diamond-point intensity of rapaciousness and compassion, a lone eagle: Fyodor Mikhailovich Dostoevsky.

I was sensationally happy at the Door, my coffeehouse on the frozen steppes of Texas—maybe even happier than Sisyphus. It's a beautiful world when the demons are reposing.

In digging around in Dostoevsky's letters I rediscovered a single passage that I committed to memory, a passage from a letter to his brother, Mikhail, on the occasion of his departure from the Peter and Paul Fortress for the prison in Siberia:

Mournful was the moment when we crossed the Urals. The horses and the sledges sank in the snowdrifts. A blizzard was raging. It was night and we had to leave our sledges and wait until they were dragged out of the snow. All around us snow was falling and the wind was howling. We were standing on the border between Europe and Asia; in front of us lay Siberia and our mysterious future and behind my past life...

The more I delved into Dostoevsky's letters, however, the deeper I probed with my trowel, the more I grubbed and gleaned and gathered, the more I learned about Fyodor Dostoevsky, the more I came to realize that my idol was not the fine and noble personage I'd imagined him to be. Again and again, in the letters, I was struck by the pettiness and triviality that Dostoevsky displayed in his private life. His plan, for example, outlined in a letter to Mikhail, to fleece his aunt Kumanina of ten thousand rubles. Again and again, in the letters, I saw the author of *Crime and Punishment* trotting to the pawnshop with watches, jewelry, even articles of clothing—anything—to get money to gamble at the roulette tables in Hamburg, Baden-Baden and Saxon-les-Bains. While working on *The Eternal Husband*, he even went so far as to pawn his trousers. This picture, that of the world-famous Dostoevsky pawning his trousers, is surreal beyond belief. I can well imagine an editor objecting, if this incident were included in a work of fiction, that it was too far-fetched. But the realm of the ignominious was in fact Dostoevsky's forte. His capacity for self-abasement was boundless, as his groveling letters to his wife, Anna, amply reveal.

Fyodor Dostoevsky was five feet, six inches tall. He smoked incessantly. He was thin and nervous; he was epileptic. He suffered from digestive upsets, probably linked to excessive drinking. He was a compulsive gambler. He was a masochist. He was impossibly disorganized and impractical. He was anti-Semetic. He was not strictly honest, not charitable, not generous, not kind, not altruistic, not magnanimous, not fine, and not noble: he was a *man*. He was at once the last true man of the nineteenth century, and the first recognizable prototype of the modern artist, the man who goes down into the abyss with a miner's lantern pinned to his hat, the man who risks everything. And yet, although he is a prototype, he has no replica, because he has no peer. They broke the mold after they made this man. He is the one and only Dostoevsky, the man who parted every veil, the supreme artist who penetrated, beyond every illusion, the very heart of darkness.

The bathroom at the Door was delightful. Leafy green

plants, Andrew Wyeth prints on the walls, old bottles turning lavender on the windowsill. The ambiance of the coffeehouse itself was militant, strident, masculine, but the bathroom was feminine. Here, for some reason, in the bathroom, the warlike aspect was abated, and the masculine aggressiveness and doctrinaire fanaticism were melted down. Bathrooms, I find, are frequently the most *human* room in any household: the flowers, the soft colors and the whimsical knick-knacks. It's as if it is only here, with the door securely bolted and our pants pulled down, that we can look on the world with anything like gentleness and benevolence.

Pablito and Barry were different from the others. I felt an affinity with them. Barry was a young minstrel from Odessa—Texas—not Russia—who played a one-stringed instrument he called a "plunker." Pablito was a flamenco dancer. It's significant in my mind that none of us— Pablito, Barry, or myself—entered into the discussions. We three were living our private myths. The others, the intellectuals, were barnacles, little clinging, sucking organisms whose one wish was to attach themselves to some hero figure. Barry—young, strong and innocent—sat at his table in the corner, smiling serenely, the Pied Piper of his own imagination, persistently plunking on his one-string and singing songs he'd made up, mostly to himself. Pablito sprawled at his table, grandly drunk, preening like a peacock, engulfed by panting admirers.

I sat at my table with my books, furiously scribbling in the margins. Sometimes it was a commentary on the text that I wrote, and sometimes it was a comment on what was taking place in the room, or in my head. For me, there was no definite boundary line where Dostoevsky left off and the Door began, or where Russia left off and Texas began. This was the secret of my happiness. I was a jade Buddha glowing with a soft interior flame. The fuel I was burning was my own substance. In this state I would sit motionless for hours, reading the same line over and over, like the aborigine who stands one-legged, hour after hour, locked in eternal dreamtime, while unheeded flies crawl freely in and out of his mouth. I was dreaming in the same way that a cockroach dreams as it crouches, feelers twinkling, in its tunnel under the wallpaper. I was an insect entranced by the thunder of the mountain god. My dreams were the dreams of Sisyphus, the dung beetle who wrestles eternally with a Fugiyama of shit.

I'm not sure, even at this distance, what I was trying to get at with my mad scribbling in the margins of those Russian novels. It had to do, needless to say, with Russia, with the greats of Russian literature, Lermontov, Gogol, Belenski, Turgenev, and the people's hero Aleksei Maksimovich Peshkov, who had the good sense to change his name to Maxim Gorky. And of course with Dostoevsky. I don't know exactly what I was trying to accomplish, but I do know that the words shot out of me like machine-gun bullets. When the margins of the books were exhausted, I turned to napkins and menus, and then to the tablecloth. Out of deference to me, Guy refrained from changing the tablecloth on "my" table, and as a result, after a month had passed, that tablecloth resembled a memorandum that Dostoevsky might have dictated to his stenographer in the midst of an epileptic seizure.

Pablito, Barry and I. We three. We sat at our tables like the Three Bears of storybook land, waiting for Goldilocks to show... Well, Pablito, of course, he had plenty of them. Pablito the flamenco dancer was far and away the brightest star in the firmament of the Door. A vigorous young Spaniard taking the Americans for everything he could get, he had the thighs of a bison. When he stomped on the stage, he cracked the two-by-fours in half, a tremendous tour de force. I remember because later, after Pablito left for LA (into the west, like the great sun itself), I made a few bucks repairing the stage. When he wasn't dancing, Pablito sat at his table downing ceramic cups of Gallo wine, tossing his curls, his eyes glinting dangerously, a real fire-breathing dragon of a man, perpetually surrounded by admirers, sweating like a bull, like one of the Karamazov brothers drunk on Wild Russian Vanya. *Sweating.* He was always sweating. The cheek of man, his fantastic bravado, the pluck of him, the set of his cap. Even his sweat was holy! Pablito was the real thing and he proved it, wrecking the stage with his boot heels. He simply dazzled the broads and the men gazed at him with stunned admiration. Pablito was a MAN, something they'd apparently never seen before, much less dreamed of being.

Guy's wife Celeste was promiscuous but she didn't notice me and I was thankful for that. I had what I wanted: a place to roost. I simply wanted to *be*. I was supremely happy in my Dostoevskian world, my White-Nights world of Mother Russia.

Of course it was Roscoe, as usual, who rocked the boat. He smashed, accidentally, Celeste's pet record, "I Hate The Capitalist System," by Sara Ogan Gunning. Then he stole a college professor's watch. This after he'd dipped in the till, as I mentioned, a misdemeanor for which Guy forgave him. But then one of the professor's disciples accused Roscoe of lifting the watch, and Roscoe, fried to the hat on Gallo wine on that particular night, and of course full of righteous indignation that somehow in his drunkenness he made seem real, denied it up and down. The stalemate raged sullenly for a few days. The night Roscoe quit, he told them off—a fine performance, dashing his ceramic wine cup into the fireplace and swinging his wet mop at the intellectuals who just *sat* there. We weren't in Mother Russia after all, I discovered. This jolt shocked me back to so-called reality. My perfect Dostoevsky world was shattered.

Notwithstanding all this, through a fortuitous circumstance (that of Guy's absence), Roscoe and I managed to slink back to the Door. Guy got busted in Guadalajara after embarking on an insanely risky drug deal which entailed hitchhiking to New Jersey to pick up a used taxi, then driving to Guadalajara, and after changing cars and getting the bricks and stashing them under the floorboards, starting back—which of course is when they nabbed him. It was a deal that had a lot of funny aspects to it. It worked fine on paper, as they say.

Celeste went down to Guadalajara by bus to visit Guy in prison. Everything was copasetic; he could have conjugal visits and there was plenty of *mota* around the place if you had the price. It was exactly the same as on the outside; you could get anything you wanted as long as you were willing to pay for it, a fact at which I suppose Guy must have laughed ironically. Guy was good at irony. But it was still jail and there were cockroaches and scorpions and he might rot there forever. But Mexico being Mexico, it was a matter of money.

So Celeste trundled the long way back by bus and staged a benefit dinner at the Door—spaghetti and meatballs, bring your own wine—the idea being to collect enough jack to spring Guy. It was a pitiful affair; I hate even to relate this, but I'm going to go through with it. She collected only twenty-seven dollars. After it was over, Celeste sat with her cigarette squashed in her plate of cold spaghetti, jawing endlessly, her eyes dead, hopeless, passing a joint. Words and more words... Talk... Crap and futility... In a way, the spaghetti dinner verified the opinion they had of life and of themselves: it was meaningless. Pablito was long gone, Barry sat serenely in the corner plunking his one-string, and the inner circle hunched around the big table discussing the matter. Did they really want to get Guy out of the slam or did they just want to talk about it? Then Celeste cried, and her mascara ran down into the spaghetti. She was so *certain* she could work it all out in her little bean. She *knew*. That's what got me, about the lot of them. They *knew*. But *what* did they know? Celeste had the world's problems neatly tied up and alphabetized in her mental filing cabinet, but she couldn't even fix a decent meal. Meanwhile Guy was dying in

Guadalajara, curled up in the dirt like a dog, his guts raging with dysentery.

To top everything off, the little fellow who was forever harping about Sisyphus insisted that we use the money we'd collected, the twenty-seven bucks, for a couple of deluxe sausage pizzas. So we did. And what about Guy, rotting in the slammer? Well, the general consensus was, after we were all stoned and drunk and stuffed with rich food, that Guy could go piss up a rope. Nobody cared, nobody really gave a rat's ass. Guy, with his shining ideas about Platonic reality and bettering the world… Where did it get him? We'd like to believe that we lead heroic lives, that like Hector and Achilles we're slain by the gods, but the truth is we die farting like bloated sausages.

"One must imagine Sisyphus happy." Well, yes, I can see it: this poor bastard deserves to be happy. I suppose it really is incumbent upon us to imagine Sisyphus happy. But what of the rest of the world's billions? Shall they be shoved aside, as always, these pathetic human sausages? No! One must imagine *everyone* happy. One must imagine a furious tide of happiness that sweeps over the billionfold army of calcified human barnacles, igniting these tiny light bulbs—suddenly and dramatically—to a star-dimming incandescence. One must imagine a pure, radiant current of happiness, a dynamo of happiness so volcanic, so savage and atavistic that it demolishes the human fuses through which it surges, spitting in its wake a farrago of charred smiles and ecstatically sputtering cinders. A murderous, irrepressible, death-dealing pianissimo chorus of happiness that ravishes like a blitzkrieg and devastates like Bubonic Plague. A shrieking firestorm of happiness that snaps the bones like toothpicks, that liquefies the flesh, that turns the blood to powder, that pulverizes the brain…

16

IT'S FUNNY how hanging out at the Gusano Club depressed me. Perhaps it was Josefina's dour, workaday presence behind the bar. Or maybe it was the mescal worm imprisoned in the tequila bottle, like a pickled fetus. In order to belong to the "club" you had to down at least one. There was nothing to it, of course. But why bother?

Another depressing thing about the Gusano Club had to do with Angel Mike, the bartender at the Navy Rose. His picture, his school athletic photo, was pasted on the front window of the Gusano Club, along with other photographs of local and national heroes, including the inevitable photograph of Francisco Pancho Villa. The first time I noticed Angel Mike's photo I looked and there he was, in sweat pants, years younger, with a white towel twisted round his throat. With him, his pals, embracing each other. It was a soccer team, fútbol. The young faces, so hopeful, so idealistic... They looked like a suicide brigade.

When, standing at the bar of the Navy Rose one night, I mentioned it to him, Angel Mike, the fútbol photograph displayed in the window of the Gusano Club, he seemed embarrassed and passed over it quickly. That was another lifetime, apparently. That was somebody else. Now his powerful athlete's body was running to blubber. He was drinking a lot at work. His eyes, couched behind pillows of fat, were red and bloodshot. He frequently needed a shave. He was already a little heavy in the jowl. He waddled. And his fingers were puffy. He was rapidly becoming the fat man he would one day be. He had reached the end of his trajectory; Angel Mike had gone as far as he could go: a bartender in a whorehouse on Mariscal Street, the Boulevard of Broken Dreams. That was the top of the heap. And now he had a family, hungry mouths to feed. There was nothing in front of him, no horizons. There was nothing left but the deadly routine. The job, the family, the job. The tortillas and the beans, packing it in. And the booze. Thank God for the booze!

During the three years I knew him I watched Angel Mike curl up like a caterpillar in a cocoon of lard, a fetus pickled in brine. I saw him passing into fat and *familia*. The process was painful and irreversible. He literally died before my eyes. Sometimes, at the Navy Rose, when things were slow, we would roughhouse and arm wrestle, just like always. But it wasn't the same. When I first met Angel Mike, I had a hard time beating him. Now I let him win, and it was getting to be a bore. He was weak as a kitten. How *easily* Angel Mike died, like a guppy. That's what I couldn't get over. He was a regular kamikaze pilot. Whenever we talked, over shots of tequila, I was bored stiff, and somehow desperately sad. His mood, I sensed, was exactly the same. He was bored, yes. He amused himself, sure—with women, with the *lotería*, with the cockfights—but it was all backing up in his throat. That much was obvious. Life was no longer any good for him. *La vida no vale nada*. Angel Mike had arrived. He had reached the famous *nada*, the Mexican ideal, the stubborn, fatalistic, and above all *defiant*, conviction that life is worthless. He *wanted* to die.

Ysela was fanatically determined to get to the US. But she refused to marry me. She figured I'd be as useless as Roscoe when it came to being a breadwinner, and I knew in my heart she was right. I knew too that the boxer would never marry her. "El Indio" Mendoza had plenty of ladies. But I had to get her across the border—somehow. A dozen more years of the Mariscal Street life, if she survived it, and her looks would be gone. She'd spend her nights in the Catacombs, sucking the pricks of young soldiers through the iron bars for a dollar or fifty cents American. *No pagas mucho, Johnny!* Ysela's cousins, Victor and Gustavo, were planning to go through the Nogales Wash, a drainpipe that connects the twin cities, Nogales, Sonora and Nogales, Arizona, and Ysela wanted to go with them, but it was a dangerous undertaking, and Monalisa advised them against it.

We were standing in front of the hut in Colonia Alta Vista, watching some half-naked children playing in the polluted creek. A scrawny chicken was pecking in the dust at our feet. Monalisa, carrying a folded newspaper, came out of the hut and joined us. She opened the newspaper and showed us the story on the front page.

"The body of an illegal immigrant who was swept away in the flooded border tunnel last week in Nogales has been recovered. Authorities identified the woman as Maria Elena Garcia, 22, of Iguala, Guerrero, Mexico. Garcia was among four people reported swept away Thursday morning. Authorities do not know what happened to the other three people. Santa Cruz County Sheriff George Eastman said sudden flash floods during the summer pose 'a real serious threat and danger' to illegal immigrants who try to cross the border through the Nogales Wash."

"Are you sure you want to do this?" I asked Gustavo. "You know what could happen…"

Gustavo nodded solemnly. "Yes, I know. If the water

comes, we die."

Victor pointed at the children playing in the polluted creek. "If we stay here, we die."

The thought of Ysela and little Lucinda drowning in that sewer scared the hell out of me. I made her promise not to go through the Nogales Wash. There was supposed to be a spot over near Zaragoza where the vigilantes were scarce and it was relatively easy to get across once the money was in place, and as my part of the bargain I promised to get a job and raise the money to pay a coyote.

The very next day Paulo informed me that the midget doorman at the Durango Club needed a letter written in English. He thought he might kick down around ten bucks American. I went by the Durango Club. The midget was standing outside, as always.

"How-do-you-do-my-friend-take-a-look-inside!" he said, swinging the door open with a flourish. When I didn't react he did a double take, and after patting me on the arm he dropped his personality. "Are you the man?" he asked me in Spanish.

"*Si, señor.*"

"How much will it cost?"

"Forget it, *cuñado*. It's a favor."

"Let me buy you a drink."

"Sure."

After a few drinks the midget said he had a job for me—a real job. It was in a factory in El Paso. They hired only Mexicans, green card workers, but the foreman, Alejandro Ruiz, was a friend of his and he was certain they'd take me on.

The job was interesting at first. Most of them are...for a day or so. The company manufactured and shipped terrazzo tabletops. The tabletops were cast and polished then stacked on pallets to be bundled in cardboard boxes—which often had to be cut to fit—then packed in wooden crates custom-made by Alejandro's crew to fit the particular item.

I was put to work making crates to specified dimensions. Now that I had a job I felt righteous and somewhat workmanlike, but I missed the afternoons in bed with Ysela.

The boss, the big white man, came around with his clipboard. "Mel." Not a bad guy. Metzger, his name was, Melvin A. Metzger. He was a big, strapping dude, an ex-college football player. He smoked a pipe and wore an English tweed workman's cap pulled down over one eye. He'd clap you on the shoulder and give you the old college pep talk, gruff but congenial, like a big friendly bear. The men, all Mexican nationals but me, seemed to like and respect him.

Our workplace was a factory warehouse, huge, dimly lit, filled with dust generated by the grinding and buffing machines. Forklifts chugged up and down narrow aisles between towering stacks of lumber and piles of machinery covered with canvas tarps. Rolls of paper and drums of oil and kerosene squatted on wooden pallets, and the terrazzo tabletops, highly polished, were stacked up like hero sandwiches with cardboard cheese slices in between.

Mel's wife, Allison, did the bookkeeping in a little office on the second floor. It was a young business on the way up. Mel put in long hours. In the evenings his wife would come round with a thermos of coffee and cheer him on. Sometimes Mel would come up to me and joke around, encouraging me to knock off for a few moments. He seemed like he wanted to tell me something but couldn't find the right words. Not that he was going to fire me... No, I was hoping for that! But he probably wanted to get things off his chest, and I was the only English speaker around besides the little woman, who was perpetually busy with the bookkeeping and correspondence. Had I permitted this relationship with Mel, he might have made a place for me in the organization, which for me would have been a much worse situation. I simply can't do that kind of work. It's too monotonous.

Mel—Melvin A. Metzger—was amicable, hardworking, avaricious and ambitious. With the men he was firm but comradely, like a good first lieutenant or a scoutmaster. He had a propensity for clowning. He'd take a football stance, crouching, knuckles brushing the concrete floor of the warehouse, then he'd charge, he'd pretend to take the ball, then he'd spin off as if eluding a tackler. His esprit de corps was high (but then it was his corps), and this enabled him to get more out of the men. Mel was a born leader but he was no slave driver. The wages were better than might have been expected and the men worked hard and willingly. I felt like a stick in the mud in this veritable hive of industrious beavers. It wasn't because I wanted to drag my heels, either. God knows I tried! But, dear Jesus, it simply wasn't in me. I knew after two weeks that I was a disappointment to Alejandro, the doorman's friend who went out on a limb to give me a shot.

Mrs. Metzger, Allison, had a crush on me; I'm pretty sure of it. She had her eye on Alejandro, too, but Alejandro was far too serious to think of dallying with *El Patrón's* wife. Sometimes on breaks I'd go upstairs and visit Allison in her cubbyhole. She was a drab little creature who pecked like a scrawny chicken at black numerals on a white page, forever clicking the keys, tallying up the receipts, balancing the budget. By way of conversation, she'd say things like, "I've got to calculate my POC entries today…" I admit I wondered what she'd be like in bed. But you'd have to have a protractor on the end of your penis to deal with a woman like Allison. She probably had an algorithm between her legs. Or a differential equation.

Alejandro, the foreman, was handsome, serious, intense, with shiny brown skin and bright, no-nonsense brown eyes that were feverish for work. He was a roving quarterback, completely in charge, scrappy, always talking it up, urging us on to further efforts. He'd grab the work from my hands, for example, knock it together with lightning speed, and then hand it back to me. It looked so easy when Alejandro did it, every movement crisp, precise, like a machine. I made the same mistakes over and over again, and each time he showed me with the same controlled fury:

"*Así.* Like this. *Me entiendes?* All the time more fast, *sabes?* These more fast, okay? More better, *si? Me entiendes? Rápido, rápido!* The fast is better, okay? Fast, fast. All the time, more fast, okay? I cannot speak to you in English, it is not my language."

Alejandro hopped from man to man, firing us up like a second lieutenant jumping from foxhole to foxhole, oblivious of whizzing shells. Each time, after Alejandro left me, I worked like a house afire, repeating to myself all the things he'd said and trying to believe it. But after I'd done a few crates, I inevitably began to slow down. Not from fatigue, but my attention began to wander. I shouldn't have been allowed to work alone. There was something missing from my psyche; I wasn't in gear. The others were in forward and I was in neutral. I was spoiled, I know that now. Living in America, and having been around the world, I learned too early in life that in this country you don't have to work to survive, and also that survival is possibly the most interesting level.

Alejandro was on a good salary. Mel recognized his value as a sparkplug. He was quite aware of Alejandro's qualities and he paid him handsomely to stay on. It was much more, for example, than he could have made at the coffin factory. That's where everybody went, from the crate factory—to the coffin factory. The coffin factory was across the state line in New Mexico, near Las Cruces, not far from Quick Draw. That was the itinerary, this was the route followed by these ambitious immigrants. The men came over from Juárez, working on green cards, they got on making crates with Metzger, they learned the trade, they developed their skills and they learned English. Meanwhile they got their papers, and then they graduated to the coffin factory in Las Cruces, where, as American citizens, they got medical benefits and vestment and the rest of it, and maybe in forty or sixty years, who knows, they could fucking well wind up as the president of a tombstone company.

I lacked enthusiasm for this program, I'll admit it, and, as I've already intimated, for the work itself. Alejandro would grab me by the arm and lead me down a dusty aisle, glancing intently at his clipboard. He'd point out a terrazzo tabletop, or a stack of three or four. "Make one crate for this. You make same way for these." Then he was gone. Working alone it was easy to dream off, which I kept doing even though I didn't intend it. Sometimes, without realizing what was happening, I'd go from making crates to making crosses, crucifixes, little sculptures, sort of. When I heard footsteps approaching, I'd hide my artwork behind the crated tabletops that were waiting to be shipped. All the while I kept thinking: Here I am at the crate factory, and I'm getting in shape for the coffin factory. That's the next stop... In my mind I could see the coffins moving down the assembly line, the workers spitting tacks, hopping like monkeys, hawking poison up out of their lungs, toiling feverishly, one with the process, cogs in the clockwork. My ears were ringing with the intense chatter of gears and rollers and conveyor belts, an enormous hum of machinery, like a hive full of bees, all in the service of death. Suddenly a pneumatic chisel falls like the blade of a guillotine. An arm is severed; it lands in an open coffin; the lid is stapled on automatically. The cunning little monkeys run around with gauze and first aid kits, sopping up the blood. Very efficient, you bastards! The formaldehyde is seeping into everything, numbing the brain, freezing the heart...

Metzger. He kept trying to get friendly. He'd give me the old college bit and I'd come back at him deadpan with, "Yes, Bwana?" I didn't want to get involved; I knew I'd only let him down. I'd seen this same situation blossom disastrously before. It was a pattern in my life. They all wanted to kick me upstairs, they wanted to do something for me, wanted to help me make something of myself. I was bored. So long! Usually I moved on without regret, but Mel was a decent guy. I didn't want to fink out on him. I felt the same about Alejandro—the Student Prince! I had only the warmest regard for Alejandro, and I honestly regretted that I couldn't become a machine just to please him.

Then, too, I needed the money. To get Ysela across the border… That was my goal, my raison d'être. I had to keep reminding myself of that, every minute, every hour, as the days stretched into weeks.

The other guys, they were princes too, Alejandro's worker pals. They were forever gathering round me, feeling my muscles. They were small and slightly built, like miniature greyhounds. They liked me and they wanted to adopt me. It was puppy love. Their sincere brown eyes, so friendly… I didn't want to take advantage of their naive friendship. They were brimming over with hope and goodwill, with a boundless enthusiasm for starting a new life in a new country. I didn't want to be the one to change their minds about America. They were too good to me, always ready to share their food when I'd forget to bring my lunch. Could they lend me a few dollars? Buy me a meal? Did I need to borrow a car for any reason? They couldn't do enough for me. My second day on the job, for example, one of the workers, Eduardo Sanchez, invited me home with him for a bath and a meal and to meet his sister.

That's the sort of man I am: the sort of man one invites home for a bath.

17

ONE NIGHT IN DECEMBER I ran into Roscoe at the Rosita Club, where traditionally, in the old days, we'd begin our sieges on Mariscal Street by drinking tequila shots and watching the bullfights on TV. Nothing like a little carnage to start things off!

Roscoe was in an abysmal state. In fact, when I walked into the Rosita Club and saw him standing at the bar, I hardly recognized him. He was thinner, much thinner, bone-thin, and more haunted than ever. He was wearing shiny, threadbare, brown gabardine pants with an incongruous knife-like crease and his toes were poking out of mangled, mismatched shoes. His blade-like wrists stuck out of the sleeves of a shit-brindle sport coat, and under the ratty sport coat was a grimy t-shirt. Fresh cuts adorned his face, and his jaw was one big black and yellow bruise. His eyes had a fishy, feverish look. He stood at the bar like a specter, clutching a tequila, gazing half into space and half at the dead TV, not really seeing me at all with that gooky stare of his as I sailed in the door. It was a strange moment. The bartender flicked at a fly with his wet rag and water trickled softly in the gutter at the foot of the bar while a few perfumed whores strolled to and from their rooms, banging the swinging door just past the *excusados*.

"How are you doing, brother?" I ventured.

We shook hands, and even then I wasn't entirely sure he recognized me. I bought him a tequila and he began to spill it out, the story of his misfortunes. Last night he'd met a girl named Serafina at El Extranjero, the Foreign Club, and it was all running off perfectly until, at four in the morning, as he was leaving the Foreign Club, he'd been rolled by three *marijuanos* and woke up in the gutter with his head resting on a frozen clod of dirt next to the wheel of a taco vendor's cart on *Calle Ugarte*, and the vendor's donkey was licking his face as the morning sunlight streamed down into his eyes, blinding him. But there was more. It had to do with his domestic situation: he'd parted the whiskers once too often, he informed me distractedly, and now Pilar was pregnant.

"That's bad..."

"No, that's good. She's knocked up, bro. And I'm sure it's mine. Funny thing... Whore that she is, or rather whore that she was, she's very moral. In fact she's too goddamn moral. I wish she could be more of a whore. Ever since we got married it's like I'm fucking a Carmelite nun. But this baby is something. This is my daughter or son. And it's mine. For once in my useless life I'm going to have something that really belongs to me. But she thinks this baby's a ticket to Los Estados Unidos for the whole damn family. And she's right. We'll get their papers. I've got no problem with that. But, what then? She thinks I'm King Midas, the man from the golden land. The land of milk and honey. And gold. Gold up the ass. I can't tell you what this cunt thinks about America..."

Since we were at the Rosita, our traditional kickoff point, and it was early evening, I suggested we do the town, but Roscoe astounded me: he said he didn't feel like it. I realized that he was probably hungry so I suggested that we go over to the American side and have a meal at the Hollywood Cafe, for old times sake. Resignedly, he agreed. On the American side, after we crossed the bridge, Roscoe automatically checked phone booth coin returns for quarters as we trudged along like priest and prisoner marching to an execution.

After *huevos rancheros* and one beer each at the Hollywood Cafe I pressed a few bills into Roscoe's hand and we parted.

Three weeks later I met Roscoe again, on the American side. Things had progressed. He was talking about killing his wife. He'd just come from the library where he'd been studying the *Encyclopedia of Crime*, A for arson, B for burglary, C for counterfeit, D for dynamite, E for electric chair, F for fugitive, G for garrote...

Again, a meal at the Hollywood Cafe was in the offing. On the way to the restaurant, as we came to a *ropa usada*, Roscoe voiced a request. He wanted to buy a necktie. We went inside, blinking our eyes to accustom them to the murky light. Roscoe picked up a striped necktie and twisted it in his hands. "Hey, you're looking good," he said to me suddenly, seeming to notice me for the first time since our meeting three weeks before at the Rosita Club. The salutation concluded, he dimmed like a bulb and plunged back into the labyrinth of his personal dilemma. For one thing, there was the nightmare tangle of red tape over the papers for the relatives...

"They treat you like shit. Once you get inside their fucking offices, you're nothing. You're just a goddamned donut frying in fat."

"Don't you think I know that?" He wasn't getting any sympathy from me!

"There's no place in this world for guys like us," he muttered bitterly, twisting the necktie in his hands and knotting it in a hangman's noose. Having established this precept as a steering block, he went on to recount the rest of his woes, Pilar pregnant, the job fallen through, the relatives from Colonia Vicente Guerrero moving back in with them, and so on.

It was a comfortable place, the used clothing store, homey and peaceful-like. While the proprietor dozed at the counter over an outdated magazine, old Mexican women poked through the bins, picking over the tangled rags, chuckling intimately and contentedly among themselves like mother hens, their brown faces creasing with joy under severe black kerchiefs as they held up baby clothing, tiny pants and shirts, and seersucker shorts with elastic leg bands. Everything was still alive in these women, clucking over a rag snatched from the dustbins and held up to gleeful scrutiny. They enjoyed themselves with complete abandon, without a shred of guilt about hitchhiking on memories.

But Roscoe of course couldn't see any of this. He was embroiled in his troubles; he couldn't escape them for a moment. He went on twisting his necktie, enumerating his difficulties. There was his poor health: his sinuses, the insomnia, and now he had a lump in his right testicle that was driving him crazy. He'd been to several doctors, and all of them diagnosed it as an enlarged blood vessel, a varicosity, nothing serious, but Roscoe wasn't satisfied, he was certain it was...he didn't want to say the word, but he couldn't stop *thinking* about it. He went from doctor to doctor, and since he had no money to pay, he kept changing his name, and he was quite inventive about it, too. From Roscoe Longworth to Rory Lampwick, for example; or Morry Lempkin, or Loris Marmont. And more variations: Lamont McCrory, Roy Larimer, Rodney Langston, Ray Long, Ross Langtree... The embryonic writer in Roscoe Longworth was coming out at last. Rodrique Langostino, Royce Ludwig, Rutger Lockridge, Ronert Lichtenstein, Rodolfe Longtemps, Rex London, Roosevelt LeRoy... He had a million of them.

Each doctor told him the same thing: a harmless varicosity. A weakened blood vessel had expanded, like a section of a worn-out inner tube. But Roscoe couldn't buy it. He wasn't convinced. What he *was* convinced of was that the lump in his balls was malignant. He was certain that his balls were rotting away, little by little, day by day. His library hours, which were normally devoted to gathering information about distant cities and mapping out escape routes, were now entirely consecrated to the avid reading of medical texts—each paragraph suggesting new symptoms. The world was closing in on Roscoe. He couldn't sleep nights. He'd used up his tabs at the cantinas on Mariscal Street, and he'd been reduced, in recent months, to cadging drinks from pimps and *braceros*, posing as a Mexican. This was the one thing that gave him pride, his ability to pass.

My third meeting with Roscoe took place in Alligator Park. He'd just come off a shoplifting spree at Woolworth's and he was elated. Triumphantly, he showed me a lipstick, a set of costume earrings and a bracelet that he intended to give to Serafina, the whore who worked at the Foreign Club. He chattered euphorically about the paranoia he'd experienced—and the exhilarating surge of adrenaline—as he made for the exit and saw those two store cops sitting on a loveseat near the door. He described the sense of triumph and personal vindication he'd felt as he steeled himself and marched past the pair in perfect control, and out onto the sidewalk, a free man.

"I left those cocksuckers sitting there on that loveseat like Tweedledum and Tweedledee!"

This time we went to Coney Island—the hotdog place, 105 Main Street, facing the park—for a meal. After we'd eaten, Roscoe's mood fell. His euphoria had been nothing more than a momentary ascent to a dizzying height. Now, with a meal under his belt, he plummeted like a murdered goose, straight to the bottom.

"It's funny about Pilar. The more we fight, the more we fuck. Otherwise she never gives me any. She really is a nun. The more I hate her, the more I love her. It's funny, you know? We've had some pretty good go-rounds lately, when we aren't trying to kill each other. Women are hotter when they're pregnant. But doesn't it burn your ass, the stuff they talk about when it's over? *Jesus!* First it was a dresser she wanted to buy, and now she's talking about new lampshades. Christ, we don't even have any electricity and she's talking about that shit. I was reading today in the library about Ilse Koch, 'The Bitch of Buchenwald.' She made lampshades out of human skin..."

We walked the streets for a while, then stopped in front of a gun shop window near Paisano, the east-west artery. Roscoe was in a frazzled state. With his sunken cheekbones and haunted eyes plunged deep in ridges of bone, and the ice-cream soft lights playing on his domed skull, his face reminded me of a photograph I'd once seen of the mad surrealist playwright Antonin Artaud, whose vision of the world was the Theater of Cruelty.

"There's the solution," Roscoe whispered feverishly, "right inside that window. Sure, that's it. I'll kill myself. But I'd rather kill *her*..."

Inside the window was a pistol with a black-tubing shoulder rest and a telescopic sight, some linked blue-tipped 20 mm shells for a Vulcan cannon, an Italian World War I helmet with a ridge on top, an array of bayonets, and a black submachine gun with a swastika on the grip. I was thinking now of Pilar, her belly swollen like a ripe melon, and inside the germinating seed that would become first a transparent flower, a delicate blossom glowing with pumping arteries and veins, then a luminous glass shrimp, then a beautiful rounded kicking fetus, an entity with arms and legs, a tiny fragile human being.

"I'll tell you what I'd like to do," Roscoe muttered. "I'd like to shove that machine gun barrel up her twat and blow her ovaries out her asshole."

When I said nothing, he again began talking about shooting himself. And when I snorted with laughter, he pretended to be hurt. "You don't think I can do it?" he snapped bitterly, clenching his fist. "You know something, Jerz, you're some kind of a friend. Here I am talking about suicide and—"

"A lot of good it does to talk," I interrupted him.

Roscoe's face fell; he spun on his heel and started walking away. I'd been thinking to jolly him out of his doomsday mood, but suddenly I saw that he was serious, or at least he made me believe he was serious, which scared the shit out of me. I caught up with him and grabbed him by the arm.

"Hey, wait a minute. I was kidding. Go ahead; get it out of your system. I'm listening."

We walked in silence around the block and paused again in front of the gun shop window.

"You've heard of these fucking crazy war heroes who walk out of their house one day with a machine gun and just start chopping away right and left. There was a guy in the paper the other day who did that. In New Orleans, I think. Boy, there're plenty of people out there like that today, hiding behind closed doors with loaded guns, peeking through keyholes, jerking themselves silly, just waiting to blow somebody's brains out. That's how they get their nuts off. Think I'm bullshitting? Take a look at the headlines. It's a jungle, bro. Every man for himself. Yessir, that's what it's coming down to. Just step out of your front door with a burp gun in your hands and cut 'em to pieces, one and all. I don't think that's so crazy. How much can a man take?"

After a long harangue about building a bomb and blowing up the world he came back to the matter of the lump in his right testicle. We stepped into the doorway of the closed gun shop and he took down his pants and showed me. The symptom was real, no question about that. But then he let me in on another desperate concern, one that loomed on his horizon like a harbinger of destruction. He'd been measuring his dick on a daily basis, he confided as he fastened his belt buckle—both length and circumference, hard and soft, and he'd been jotting down his findings in a little black notebook. This, over a period of months.

"I've lost an eighth of an inch since September," he muttered, almost in tears. He was completely serious. He was dead certain that his cock was being eroded by cancer. "If it goes," he proclaimed, "I know I'll kill myself..."

Three months passed. I dropped by the Gusano one night and learned a sad bit of news: Felisa was dead. She'd bled to death following an abortion performed by a *curandera* who lived in the Colonia Palo Chino, a woman called "La Matadora" who worked her magic with a sharpened coat hanger and a jar of alcohol.

Josefina, behind the bar, was halfway friendly for a change. Perhaps sorrow had softened her attitude toward me. I bought her a drink, and after we'd talked for a while about old times, she came up with another item. Roscoe, she said, had vanished. It had been a month, at least, since anyone had seen him. Pilar had heard nothing, nor was there any word of him in the cantinas. He'd packed none of his belongings, no clothing, no toothbrush. His books, his journals, his framed photograph of Dostoevsky—all that was intact in the house on Prospect Street.

Josefina handed me Roscoe's copy of *The Decay of the Angel* by Yukio Mishima. "I thought maybe you might want to keep this," she said.

The consensus was, among the family, and among the bartenders and the girls in the cantinas, that Roscoe had disappeared into Mexico, had changed his identity, perhaps even his appearance. It sounded plausible enough. Roscoe's Spanish was fluent. He passed easily in the cantinas. It may well have been that the burden of family life, together with the strain of his impossible involvements, was simply too much for him, that he saw no alternative but to simply abdicate, that anything—even, and perhaps especially, a life of poverty and anonymity—seemed preferable to the excruciating complexities and entanglements of his personal melodrama. Roscoe had often told me, I recalled, that in order to solve his problems he would have to *become someone else*. In any case, and whatever the truth of the matter, I never saw Roscoe Longworth again.

18

A WEEK OR SO AFTER THE WAKE, Ysela and I went for a walk by the polluted creek that flows through Colonia Alta Vista. When we returned to the hut, we discovered that little Lucinda, left alone, had gotten into her mother's makeup kit. She was sitting on Felisa's milk crate, gazing in the fragment of mirror taped to the wall, singing sweetly to herself as she painted her face with garish colors. Lucinda looked exactly like a miniature Felisa, a "perfect little whore."

Ysela, horrified, grabbed Lucinda's shoulders and shook her.

"No, no, no, no!"

This incident seemed to portend Lucinda's future, which was fortunately averted when, some time after that, Josefina married her cowboy and immigrated to the US, Wichita Falls, taking Bebé Linda and little Lucinda with her.

I had fun picturing Josefina in shorts and a halter, pushing a loaded shopping cart, grabbing items from the aisles: Oreo Cookies, Chef Boyardee Spaghetti and Little Debbie Honey Buns. Or in a smart black dress, getting out of a Chevy Nova and handing the keys to a valet, then disappearing into the Chart House. Or the three of them, Josefina, the baby and little Lucinda, lazing in the pool, and Daryl Rivers sprawled in a plastic lounge chair with a Pabst Blue Ribbon, muttering, "You know somethin', honey, I'm *tahrd*. I mean, I'm *tahrd*…"

And things were heating up again with Ysela. As I was leaving the wake that day, Ysela arrived in a taxi, alone. She squeezed my hand and whispered tearfully, "*Te quiero*. I love you, *mocoso*," then disappeared into the hut. *Te quiero!* Those two little words. I believed her this time. And she called me "*mocoso*." I'd recently seen on TV at the Rosita Club that Juan "El Indio" Mendoza had lost his last two bouts and had crashed his Aston Martin Rapide into a tree. It was all over the papers, too. He was definitely on his way out.

And so it began once again, the spider dance, a fanged waltz around a sticky web with the Tarantula Woman, lover and cannibal, mistress and murderer of dreams.

Because Ysela was obsessed with her past lives, she insisted that I investigate my past lives too, and she made a date for us with a medium, a *curandera* who lived in Colonia Palo Chino. I wasn't all that interested in my past lives, since I couldn't seem to do much with my present one, but of course I was curious to see what was in the tea leaves for Ysela and myself, so when the day arrived we took a taxi to Colonia Palo Chino.

Señora Salvatierra, a Huichol Indian woman with a weathered but beautiful face, sat opposite us on the dirt floor of her hut. Flickering candles illuminated bundles of dried herbs hanging from the ceiling. A pet tarantula paced in its cage.

Señora Salvatierra spoke first to Ysela: "A new world awaits you, my daughter. Soon you will go on a long journey. After a difficult passage, you will reach a better land. Then all this will seem like a dream."

"The new world…"

"The new world, yes. The new world is a golden land

where the people live like deer in a forest. The trees are heavy with ripe fruit. There is plenty for all. You will eat your fill and rest in the sunshine."

"Yes..."

"For many years now it has been raining in your heart. Isn't that so?"

"Yes, yes..."

"Ah, but soon your lips will drink from a spring of the purest water."

"Yes. Oh, yes…"

"You are very religious. That is good. You have a friend in the spirit world. You do not know her but she knows you. She knows your heart. She knows your soul. She knows your suffering because she too has suffered. She reaches out her hand to you, to guide you on your journey."

"Is it far, the new world? Is it far? How soon...?"

"No, not far. Not far... And soon, very soon. Go now, little warrior. Your feet, the feet that have marched through fire, will soon be dancing in a field of flowers."

Ysela stood up and thanked the Señora, then Señora Salvatierra said to Ysela: "I am going to speak to your friend in English."

"*Muy bien*," Ysela replied. "I will wait outside."

The tarantula had stopped pacing, I noticed. He was cleaning his fangs, with a dreamy expression in his eight tiny eyes. Maybe he was dreaming of a better world.

"You are Germanic, are you not?" Señora Salvatierra asked me as soon as we were alone.

"Yes."

"And Irish?"

"Yes."

"Would you like to ask me a question?"

"Yes. Who was I in my past life?"

"Which one? There have been many."

"Any one."

"You were a soldier, a peasant, a tradesman. Many

times."

"That's not very exciting."

"Yes. That is your fate, you see. You would like to be a king, an emperor, a powerful magician. But that can never be. You are made out of the wrong sort of material. You are a peasant. You would make a wonderful Eskimo. Unfortunately, at this time in history, the world does not need your type of man. You are an anachronism. Your salvation, however, is that you are an artist. You must understand this. What you want cannot be achieved in the theater of reality. The best policy for you would be to relinquish your ambitions. They cannot be realized in this world. Become a gardener, become a sage—become Japanese! But you cannot do that, because of your stubbornness and your fatalism. You are a German and an Irishman, combined, a fanatic and a mystic, a disciplinarian and a poet, a soldier and a peasant. Compromise—the way of the sage—is alien to you. You would rather storm the gates of Heaven, or die in the mud with a bayonet between your teeth. No surrender! That is your motto, is it not? Answer me."

"Yes, it is. Yes, yes."

"You are drowning in the soul. If you do not gain control of your life you will flow back to the source, back to the matrix, without ever having left your mark on the world. One thing more: this woman, Ysela. She is a spider. She will certainly devour you. But I think you already understand that. There. Our talk is over. Please leave now. We shall not speak again."

As the weeks passed I began to wonder if Roscoe might have holed up over in Quick Draw. I had a weekend off so I took a bus over that way. The driver was surprised when I announced that I wanted to get off at Quick Draw, and he told me I'd have to flag the bus down on the way back.

Everything was the same, the boarded-up gas station, the battered Coke machine, the lonely sign that read:

"Welcome to Quick Draw, pop. 174." It was a long walk down the dirt road, and no Shep came trotting out to greet me. I knocked on the door. No answer. The silence made my ears ring. I went inside. The old house was deserted. Luther's empty chili pot squatted on the stove. His big spoon hung on the kitchen wall. A noise made me jump. It was the back door flapping in the wind. I walked through the empty house and peered out at a giant tumbleweed skidding along, bounding in huge looping arcs across the desiccated land.

Out back, near Luther's shriveled-up bean field, I found a crude wooden cross and a hand painted sign: "Shep." The old man had buried his only friend and then vanished into the desert. The desert had swallowed him up. Or else the sun had baked him like a raisin and the wind had blown him away. Quick Draw was now an official ghost town.

The pump in the back yard by the bunkhouse still worked, I discovered. Lizards skittered in the dry weeds at my feet as I pumped the handle and scooped up some water in my cupped hand. It tasted like sulfur. I realized that I was hungry. In the kitchen cupboard I found a few cans of corned beef hash and a box of instant grits. I heated the stuff up and got it down. It did the job but it sure didn't hold a candle to Luther's homemade chili.

It was too late now for the bus so I spent the night in the bunkhouse. The wind, whistling through the loose boards, kept me awake. Or maybe it was the ghost of Cherokee George, cut down in the prime of life by Texas gunslinger John Wesley Hardin. Outside, I sensed, vultures were circling. They were waiting for me to die. They were waiting for everything to die. The land was theirs, this desiccated coyote-lonely land, a habitat suitable only for saints and Gila monsters.

The coffin factory was out there, too, somewhere in the darkness, on the road to Las Cruces.

On the bus the next day I caught up on my sleep, and I

had a dream. Zihuananejo: a gorgeous open-air market, mangoes, papayas and piles of roasted goat heads. I watched a ragged Indian man—serape, straw sombrero, huaraches—as he shambled toward the market, a burlap sack slung over his shoulder. Then I was sitting in a skiff, being towed by a great green turtle. A moment later I saw the man with the burlap bag again. He was sitting on a curb, eating a goat's head. The man was Roscoe. He was relaxed, nonchalant, perfectly at home.

At the job I was getting good with the crates now, nearly good enough for the coffin factory. I still had problems with measuring, however. Very often, no matter how many times I measured and re-measured, I'd cut off too much and the board would come up short when it got to the nailing stage. I hid my mistakes—there were a lot of them—under piles of lumber where not even the sharp brown eyes of roving quarterback Alejandro Ruiz could find them.

The nest egg I kept under my mattress was growing. From payday to payday I sat on it like a mother hen. That egg was Ysela's future. We were going to hatch her a new life on the American side. But I was nervous. About Nogales, I mean, the Nogales Wash. Ysela was impulsive. An article had appeared recently in *El Diario*. Three more *mojados* had drowned trying to go through the Nogales Wash, the *cloaca* of the universe. I made Ysela promise once again that she attempt to cross, as planned, at Zaragoza, and not, under any circumstances, at Nogales. She agreed and I gave her the cash, better than a thousand bucks. I know it sounds pricey, but the package included food and water and a safe house on the American side. Plus the coyotes have to pay off the Mexican cops. Anyway, everything was decided, and I felt proud of myself.

On the day before the Zaragoza crossing I accompanied Ysela to the little temple in Colonia Alta Vista, where she knelt and prayed to the Virgen de la

Soledad.

"Holy Virgin of Soledad, give me your holiest blessings. I go now to make a better life. My Virgin Mother, I beg your permission on my knees. For many years it has been raining in my heart, but soon my lips will drink from a spring of the purest water…"

But that very night a bad omen popped up, and I couldn't get it out of my mind: *La Llorona*. Ysela went for a walk by the polluted creek, and when she came back she was spooked. I tried to get out of her what was wrong, but she clammed up on me. Gustavo and I took a walk by the creek and I pressed him for an answer.

"What's the matter with Ysela?" I asked. "She won't tell me anything."

"She thinks she saw *La Llorona*. Now she is afraid."

"Where? Where did she see *La Llorona*?"

"Right here, by the water."

"*La Llorona*… Do you mean *El Cucuy*? Who is *La Llorona*?"

It turns out that seeing *El Cucuy* is one thing. *El Cucuy* is a child's demon, a somewhat comical boogeyman that frightens little kids like Lucinda so their parents can make them behave. But seeing *La Llorona* is serious business.

"*La Llorona* is a spirit. Many years ago she was angry with her husband, so she drowned her children in the Rio Bravo. Now she cries for them, for her dead children. If you see *La Llorona*, it means you are going to die. I mean, if you believe it."

"Does Ysela believe it? Does she believe it?"

"I don't know…"

The next morning I called Allison and said I was sick. She was sweeter than a pecan praline and let me off the hook. I went directly to the Navy Rose to await some word. Rain was coming down hard, accompanied by lightning and thunder. There were no customers. Paulo and I played dominoes and drank tequila shots. We sent out for *machaca*, and the guy from the restaurant had just brought the plates when Glorieta burst through the swinging doors, wearing the same frilly red taffeta dress he'd sported at Paulo's birthday party. His dress was drenched and rain had streaked his mascara. He looked a fright. After snatching off his sopping pink-blonde wig, he informed us that the Zaragoza crossing had been delayed, due to the rain and because the coyote was waiting for a family from Guatemala who were to join the party. Before he hastily replaced the wig I realized with a start that Glorieta was bald.

"They have gone to Nogales," he blurted in a deep baritone voice. "It is very dangerous in the rain."

"It is suicide," Paulo concurred.

They were traveling in a green "*Servicio Particular*" truck with one door missing, Glorieta added.

"How long ago? When did they leave?"

"Two hours, *señores*."

What to do? Nobody had a car, and a taxi was out of the question. I went to the door and peered into the street. It was raining harder than ever. *Call Dr. Umberto*, I said to myself.

Thirty minutes later Dr. Umberto, sporting a traditional Spanish matador's hat, pulled up beside me on the American side of the International Bridge in his battered black Jaguar. He jumped out of the car and we shook hands and embraced.

"My friend, it's good to see you. I'm just sorry it had to be under these circumstances."

We got into the car and took off.

"*Jefe*, how are you?" I pumped his hand again. "How was your trip? And how is…what was her name?"

"Tizanzia DeForrest-Gallant? Is that who you mean?"

"Yes, Tizanzia DeForrest-Gallant."

"She abandoned me in Trieste for a Formula One driver. A young guy… You know these Italians! But Italy is magnificent. Rome, Venice, Napoli…"

"See Florence and die! And the book?"

"The book? Ah, yes, *Short Men in History*. Yes, one reviewer called it an engrossing...what was it? Yes, an engrossing study. Groundbreaking, I believe he said. Groundbreaking and comprehensive."

"Wonderful..."

Right after we made Lordsburg we got stuck at a railroad crossing. It was the longest freight I've ever seen. As rain whipped down, lightning flashed and thunder rumbled, blending with the rattle of the boxcars. I had a bad feeling now. I wanted to be on that train, free as a breeze, going anywhere.

The train stopped, blocking our path. We couldn't go around. Cars were stacked up behind us.

"My God, *Jefe*..."

"I know, I know. I'm doing my best."

"I know. I'm sorry..."

Once we began rolling again, Dr. Umberto really put his foot in it. He kept the Jaguar's engine wound up tight and passed everything on the road.

But the rain...

"The rain, *Jefe*. It's getting worse. The tunnel will be flooded."

"Agreed. But don't worry, my friend. We'll make it. Highway 2 in Mexico is a bad stretch of road. You know that as well as I do. We'll be there before they will, hands down."

I wasn't so sure. They'd had a good two-hour start on us. And we'd lost half an hour at Lordsburg.

When we skidded to a halt on the American side of the Nogales Wash muddy water was gushing out of the tunnel. La Migra had already arrived, three cars. Six officers in yellow slickers were poised at the tunnel entrance, grabbing and cuffing half-drowned immigrants as they came staggering out. Presently, Victor emerged, carrying Gustavo—alive or dead, we couldn't tell. We got out of the car and tried to approach, but one of the officers drew his gun.

"Manos arriba!"

"We're American citizens," Dr. Umberto protested.

"No se mueve! Manos arriba!"

"Better get 'em up, *Jefe*," I muttered. I raised my hands, and so did Dr. Umberto, belatedly, after another barked order from the officer.

Another officer led us to a squad car, patted us down and put us in the back.

Just then Ysela stepped out of the tunnel, choking and spitting water, but alive. The squad car window was closed, so I couldn't hear her scream, but I saw her mouth move as she threw herself on the ground next to the body of her cousin.

Moments later they were leading her away, along with Victor and other survivors who had been captured. They would be interrogated briefly and sent back across the border.

The officer who had told us to get our hands up came over and tapped on the front window of the squad car, and the driver rolled down the window an inch or two.

"Hey Huey, you got any more of them butterscotch drops?"

"All gone, Roy," the driver said. "Sorry. I'll bring some more tomorrow."

After Gustavo's death Ysela began descending deeper and deeper into her own darkness. She was angry with God because she hadn't drowned in the sewer with Gustavo. And she now believed that her "friend in the spirit world" that Señora Salvatierra had spoken of was none other than La Llorona, the angel of death. Our bouts in the sack were becoming more and more violent. She goaded me into abusing her. I'd give her a few black and blue marks, but not nearly enough to suit her. She wanted me to beat the shit out of her. It's simply not my cup of tea.

We were drinking a lot, too. We'd wake up in the

afternoon and start nipping on a bottle of gin or whiskey. First we'd drink to the Aztec *pulque* god, Tepoztecal, who saw the face of a rabbit in the moon and split the holy agave with a lightning bolt; then we'd drink to Francisco Pancho Villa, liberator of the poor. We drank to Benito Juárez and we drank to Mayahueti, the Olmec maiden who milks the precious *aguamiel* from the sacred cactus. I was drinking to forget that we were breaking up, and Ysela was drinking to make herself sad. She was drinking from a deep reservoir of *aguamiel* buried in the burning desert, an immense buried reservoir of sorrow, fermented from the star-crossed fatalism of the Aztecs and mixed with the Spaniard's mystical love of death.

We'd start out drinking at home, and once we'd caught a pretty good buzz we'd find a quiet booth at the Rosita Club and pound the ten-cent tequilas. One afternoon at the Rosita, Ysela, grandly drunk, smashed a Cruz Blanca bottle on the edge of our table and deliberately cut her hand with the jagged glass. She stood up, dipped her finger in the blood flowing from her hand and wrote the word "*Puta*" on her forehead in big red letters.

"This blood is not my blood only," she murmured. "This is my sister Felisa's blood. An army of men marched between her legs and she died in the dirt like a dog."

I got back on at Ling Po, the Chinese joint. The Zaragoza plan had fizzled, and the Nogales Wash, but I now had the idea of saving some cash so Ysela and I could start a new life in Zihuatanejo.

That dish room at Ling Po was the hottest place on earth, a regular steam bath. It's no fun being a dishwasher. You wear a rubber apron, a badge of shame that means you're the lowest ranking employee. The busboys bring you the dishes in bus tubs. You scrape the food into a trash barrel, load the cups, bowls and silver on a rack and spray everything off with a pressure hose. You feed the rack into the dish machine, pull the door shut, and the dish machine does its thing. It's a hard job and a thankless one.

The line cooks and the servers get all the glory, and no waitress in her right mind would dream of flirting with the dishwasher. What you hope for is a decent dish machine and a great high-pressure hose, and you hope not to pull the dinner shift.

I was friendly with one of the cooks. I'd place an order for the Schezwan Shrimp and he'd sneak it to me in a bus tub hidden under plates. If you did things the legitimate way, you got half off on the meals, which was still pretty decent. I'd always order my favorite, the Egg Drop Soup. Egg Drop Soup is a meditation, a mantra, because there's something almost cosmic and certainly very conducive to dreaming about the way the filaments of egg white swirl in the bowl like a miniature spiral galaxy with a halo of stars and a black hole in the center. It's beautiful. One minute you're sitting at the help's table at Ling Po gazing into your Egg Drop Soup and the next minute you're eating lobster under a thatched roof palapa while a marimba band plays on shore. Or you're crouching in a shark fisherman's skiff far out in Magdalena Bay where the great green sea turtles paddle to the surface then slowly sink to unimaginable depths. And in Mulegé the bare-breasted women are washing their hair in the jungle river that flows into Bahia de la Concepción between two towering palms…

But I was kidding myself. About Zihuatanejo, and about Ysela too, of course. She was getting tired of me. Worse yet, Juan "El Indio" Mendoza made a surprise comeback. You simply couldn't keep that guy down on the canvas. He beat Pepe Hernandez in Madrid, a complete upset, then chalked up two more quick wins, both by KOs in the early rounds. El Indio was on a roll. His driver would pick up Ysela in a Cadillac and whisk her away to his hotel. Ysela had no illusions about a long-term relationship with Mendoza—certainly not marriage—and she was at least halfway sold on my idea of getting the hell out of Juarez. But weeks went by and we didn't leave for Zihuatanejo. We couldn't extricate ourselves from the life on the Mariscal Street merry-go-round. The velvet octopus wouldn't release its tentacles.

19

I CAME INTO SOME CASH. My maiden aunt in Vermont heard I was trying to be a writer and sent me three hundred dollars. I decided that a little vacation was in order. I now had an opportunity to get away from Ysela and to stop thinking about her, if I could. I'd realized by this time that she wasn't about to pick up and go to Zihuatanejo with me, so I would go to Zihuatanejo alone. Zihuatanejo! The Real Mexico…

I knew it was foolish, this business about "the Real Mexico." What I wanted was to get away from Ysela and away from the border for a while. I wanted to hear Spanish spoken exclusively. I wanted to sit at the foot of a mountain on the terrace of a café where the waiter brings your tequila sunrise an hour or two after you've forgotten you ordered it. I wanted to listen to the soft melodious tinkle of Spanish in my ears, Spanish and only Spanish. I wanted to immerse myself—in Spanish, in forgetfulness, in anonymity. In Mexico you don't have to *be* anybody, you don't have to *do* anything to prove that you're worthy to draw breath. You simply *are*. And people congratulate you for it. It's enough, it suffices, it satisfies. To be, to exist. In Mexico it's a triumph, a victory. It's something to be glad about.

The day I got the check from Aunt Mizpah I went to the Tango Club to think things over. I rarely went to the Tango Club, and only then because of the music. They had Edith Piaf on the jukebox. The girls wore phantom leather jackets, black lipstick, high boots and short skirts. They were loud, coarse, stunning. Most of the clientele were *Alemánes*, German NATO exchange officers stationed at Fort Bliss, arrogant shits who dressed like European hoodlums. The rest were American doggies. I was the only one who didn't fit, as usual. The Tango Club was a rotten hole in the wall, and I hated it—except for the music.

At the Tango Club I had a few Carta Blancas and played Piaf, *"Toujours Aimer."* I tried to get the attention of one of the fluff-girls, a sullen little number with a black leather vest and an Iron Cross nestled between her tits, but she gave me a contemptuous glance and spat on the floor. Meaning that she preferred to wait for one of the storm troopers, a Kraut with a big bankroll and a big schwantz.

I ordered another Carta and glanced again at Aunt Mizpah's letter:

"Dear Jerzy, the ice is melting on Lake Bomoseen..."

I finished my beer and left the Tango. I bought a bottle of Cuervo Gold and checked into a hotel on Avenida Juárez. I could afford it, certainly, and I wanted some peace and quiet in which to mull things over—about the trip, I mean—my prospective journey to the Real Mexico.

In my room I poured myself a drink. After one drink I decided to take a bath. In the bathtub I reread a passage I'd underlined in a book I'd been carrying around with me, *The Maze and the Minotaur* by John Calvin Ryder:

"The unraveling of the thread that leads to the heart of the labyrinth is a journey of rediscovery. The clues that we vaguely recognize, the handwriting on the walls, the tentative fingers that point and crumble to dust, are emblems of a circuitous voyage. Our destination is secret, but not unknown. The course is uncharted, yet certain and fixed. The answer that we seek is not distant, but near.

The equation is simple rather than complex. The Minotaur—and the maze itself—are nothing more than an elaborate subterfuge that we have invented in order to disguise the obvious. It is as if we must circumnavigate the globe in order to arrive at our own doorstep."

Interesting, very interesting. Somehow my mood for going to Zihuatanejo had fled. For one thing, I was dead tired. I'd hardly slept the previous night, fretting about Ysela and trading punches in my mind with "El Indio" Mendoza. Maybe after a night's sleep, I told myself, turning a page. But I knew the danger of that. If I waited a day I'd hook up again with Ysela, we'd go on a spree, the three hundred dollars would be gone, and goodbye Zihuatanejo. So I got out of the tub, dried off and got dressed. *Zihuatanejo, here I come!*

On the way to the bus station I stopped at a *farmacia* to buy a new toothbrush, my only luggage besides my bottle of Jose Cuervo and *The Maze and the Minotaur*. Clothes? I'd buy a change of clothes when I got there, I told myself, something sporty, something tropical. But when I arrived at the station I discovered that it was still five hours until the next bus for Zihuatanejo, so I stepped into the street. *Five hours to kill.*

I considered going back to the hotel, but then I remembered that I'd already checked out. I knew one thing. I had a wad of bills that was burning a hole in my pocket. Suddenly, I realized I was lost. I'd been wandering aimlessly, *thinking*. The crooked streets, the leering huts, the serape-bundled figures, the smoking fires—all had been daubed by a madman with a few quick brush strokes on a muddy canvas. The cadmium yellow moonlight flowed like rich gravy over the roofs of the houses. In the rutted streets it glowed with the texture of burlap.

Gradually, I realized that I was headed south on the road toward Colonia San Felipe del Real, eventually to intersect Sixteenth of September Street. Off to my left was the sprawl of Ciudad Juárez; behind me lay the glittering bowl of El Paso surmounted by the gigantic stone Christ,

El Cristo Rey, his outstretched arms piercing the tall plumes of black smoke rising from Smeltertown.

I paused and reread the passage from Ryder, as if I were consulting a map.

"*The clues that we vaguely recognize, the handwriting on the walls, the tentative fingers that point and crumble to dust, are emblems of a circuitous voyage...*"

Emblems of a circuitous voyage... Great title! I jotted it down, on the back of Aunt Mizpah's letter.

Then I remembered. This was the route I followed from Colonia Alta Vista to Mariscal Street, in the early days, when I was living at Monalisa's with Roscoe and the in-laws. It wasn't a direct route, by any means, but it was a definite one. I went the same way every time. There were certain landmarks, certain huts that differed, however slightly, from the others, certain junctions where I turned, doglegged, zigzagged. And there were faces, young girls, very shy, who lived with their families, but staring, whenever I walked past, always in certain windows, saying everything with their eyes. In Mexico, it's the eyes that predominate. In Mexico, everyone is *watching*.

"*The course is uncharted, yet certain and fixed.*"

I plunged headlong into the maze of mud huts, striking out at first in the general direction of Mariscal Street, but then, on impulse, I began purposely making wrong turns, going down streets I'd never walked before, places I'd never been. In my mind was the image of the labyrinth; in the center, the Minotaur's lair. Never had Juárez seemed so mysterious, so hallowed, as if each adobe hut were a transparent skull lit up by a single feverish candle. Ciudad Juárez was the holy city, a citadel, more magical and shimmering than New Jerusalem. I was beginning to hallucinate from lack of sleep, and I was enjoying every minute of it.

A few hours later I was standing at the bar of a cantina on the edge of the red-light district with a tequila in my paw and my wad of bills bursting like a nugget of radium in my pocket. In my mind, I was walking the cobblestones of Zihuatanejo. I was in Ixtapa, sitting with Aunt Mizpah by the pool at the Hotel El Presidente, and the sun was shining. The tray of iced drinks arrived, and the nachos and *jalapeños* and the chilled slices of papaya bathed in lime juice. I saw the stone arches of Cabo San Lucas rising up out of the ocean like gates to the Sea of Cortez. I was eating lobster under a thatched-roof palapa while a marimba band played on the shore. I saw the lean-tos of the shark hunters at Magdalena Bay, and the great green sea turtles. And in Mulegé, the bare-breasted women were washing their long silky hair in the jungle river that flows into Bahia de la Concepción. Mexico, the Real Mexico. It's beautiful. *And I've still got five hours until I catch the bus...*

Moments later, walking again, I paused at La Calle Noche Triste, the Street of the Sad Night, such an inviting spot that one almost feels an obligation to loiter. Leaning against a pockmarked wall under a torn bullfight poster, facing the cathedral, I watched an American crossing the street. I recognized that walk. And he was carrying a folded newspaper. It was Roscoe. I was certain of it. Instinctively, I ducked into a doorway. Seconds later, peering around a *"Dentista"* sign, I watched the man, who looked nothing at all like Roscoe, disappear into a bar.

Hallucinations...

A few steps further and I found myself in front of the Restaurant Palenque, where hundreds of naked chickens were roasting on spits over troughs brimming with yellow grease. The menu was painted in red letters on the window. An exhaust fan whirled above the door, pumping heavenly aromas into the street. Inside, women in papery white dresses were rolling balls of dough on wooden boards and patting them into tortillas. Behind the women enormous ovens breathed like ravenous beasts. Sumptuous roasts and stupendous joints of fragrant roasted meat dangled on hooks among black iron pots and copper pans while doll-like *meseras* hurried with gigantic platters of chicken, roasted pork and *cabrito*. Mexico is a workers' epic, a renaissance of the senses, a folk-opera dedicated to the belly.

I buy a taco from a pushcart vendor. Leaning against a wall, I reread Aunt Mizpah's letter. Suddenly, I'm in Vermont, sitting at Aunt Mizpah's kitchen table. It's late summer—no, it's autumn, the leaves are turning to crimson and orange and the perch are biting like crazy at Lake Bomoseen. The Franklin stove is glowing cherry red and I've just finished cleaning the fish. We're drinking hard cider and Aunt Mizpah is writing me one of her long literary letters which she doesn't have to send because I'm there with her, with Aunt Mizpah, in Green Vermont.

"The Minotaur—and the maze itself—are nothing more than an elaborate subterfuge that we have invented in order to disguise the obvious. It is as if we must circumnavigate the globe in order to arrive at our own doorstep."

Walking again, along *Calle Ugarte*. Here the bricks, softly eroded like weathered bread, are slimed over with a thin plaster-wash of bile-green paint. Pushcarts squat on automobile tires in the rutted mud, and beggar children huddle in front of tiny *loncherías* whose menus are chalked on slates propped outside the door.

Calle Ugarte—I feel it through the middle, in the solar plexus—a tunnel that pierces my navel. *Calle Ugarte* is an umbilical street that connects me in an alimentary way, in a flesh-and-blood way, with Mexico. On *Calle Ugarte*, Mexico is alive. Mexico the garbage scow, Mexico the fountain of inhuman longings, Mexico, a sow with a billion tits. Mexico, Mother of the World. Mexico! *Mexico siempre!*

Of course I missed the bus. At some moment during the night I remembered. I made it to the station, but the bus had already pulled out.

"How long until the next bus?" I inquired at the window.

"Five hours, señor."

Of course! Five hours, señor!

Needless to say, I went back to Mariscal Street. More Carta Blancas, more frenzied wandering through the passageways of the labyrinth. At some ungodly hour of the morning, as though I'd been drawn there by unconscious design, blindly unraveling some finespun thread, I found myself once again in front of the Tango Club. Was this the heart of the maze? The Minotaur's lair? I sauntered inside. The place was dead, except for a single German officer seated at the bar and a humpbacked flower vendor sleeping in a booth near the toilet. The whores were waiting in a row, slumped against the wall, sullenly asleep. As I approached the bar, the German swiveled on his stool. He had a shaved head and a bull neck.

"*Wie geht's?*" he muttered, his eyes ice-blue slots in a mask. As he slid off his stool I noticed that he was a little shorter than I am, but terrifically compact and muscular. I had the distinct impression that he was inhumanly powerful—and utterly merciless.

"*Wie geht's?*" I responded, automatically shaking his proffered hand. I'm was on my toes, ready for action, but the German, after surveying me for a moment with those edelweiss eyes, smiled enigmatically and returned to his stool.

"A drink for my *Amerikaner* friend," he said to the bartender. "*Was mochten Sie trinken?*"

"*Eine tequila mitt limón, bitte,*" I managed.

I realized now why I'd returned to the Tango Club. Standing with one foot resting on the brass rail, I surveyed the lineup of girls. After deliberating for a moment, I chose one in a short black skirt with pleats, high shiny boots, and an unzipped black phantom leather jacket spangled with *Luftwaffe* emblems and the inevitable Iron Cross dangling between her breasts.

Scrumptious!

I walked over and gave her a nudge, silently holding out a crisp ten-spot.

"*Wie geht's?*"

"Kiss my ass, *guero*."

"I intend to, *meine schatz*," I answered calmly.

My excitement mounted as she coldly took the bill and went to the bar where the bartender was snoozing, rag in hand, behind the cash register. As he sleepily rang up the sale and handed her a roll of toilet paper and a token to put on her key ring, she yawned and stretched, arching her back; she glared at me over her shoulder, then spat on the floor. She was obviously pissed off at being disturbed, not at all in the mood, which excited me even more.

It was gorgeous. I made her leave everything on, the boots, the pleated skirt, the black leather jacket half-unzipped with the Iron Cross nestled between her breasts. While I strained and sweated, she coldly snapped her bubblegum and cursed me bitterly in Spanish, English and German. At the last possible instant I pulled out and came all over her tits, on her face, on her glossy black lipstick, and on the phantom leather jacket spangled with *Wehrmacht* insignia, dangling Hitler *Jungund* medals and silver swastikas. A dirty trick, but I was looking for my ten bucks worth, and I got it.

"*Pinche guey!* Motherfucker! *Cochino marrano!*"

After this treat I sat at a table and ordered a tequila sunrise, as well as a drink for the Kraut at the bar. I fed the jukebox, Piaf, the Sparrow of the Streets, warbling "*Toujours Aimer*." It's beautiful, I thought. *Nothing like this in Vermont!*

Street photographers and beggars strolled past the door, and the Menudo Man, with his steaming kettle and his wooden yoke. I kept depositing my dimes and nickels in the machine, and Piaf's magic voice came soaring out, showering despair and absolution on the early morning pavement.

A hunchback approached me, the flower vendor I'd seen earlier snoozing in the booth near the toilet. I gave the man a ten-dollar bill and told him to go to a nearby restaurant. "Bring three breakfasts," I told him in Spanish.

The hunchback had his son with him, a stunted, dreamy-eyed boy. The man's eyes, when I whipped out that ten-spot, were like saucers. I didn't know whether he'd come back or not, and I didn't care.

An hour later, after I'd forgotten all about the incident, the hunchback brought the plates, *machaca*, heaps of fried potatoes, salad, *refritos*, tortillas and a big bowl of salsa fresca. We all pitched in, the man, the boy and I, dipping our tortillas in the same bowl of salsa. The hunchback eyed me gratefully, as if I were don Benito Juárez himself, while the boy grinned foolishly and ate with his fingers.

Before I'd finished eating I told the bartender to bring me a telephone. I dialed the bus station.

"*A qué hora sale el camión para Zihuatanejo?*" I barked into the receiver. "When is the next bus for Zihuatanejo?" I felt like a *Gran Señor* with all that money in my pocket. It was exhilarating. *Money talks and bullshit walks!*

The answer came back, the answer I'd been expecting, the answer I knew I would receive:

"*Five hours, señor.*"

I bought the bartender a tequila and spread my bills out on the table. I knew I was being scrutinized by the German Minotaur at the bar, but I didn't give a rat's balls.

There it was—everything I had left, one hundred and ninety-five dollars, my vacation in Zihuatanejo. But I knew I wasn't going. I didn't have to leave because I'd already arrived. I was there...in Mexico, the Real Mexico, where the sky is always blue and the tablecloths are white and the silverware always tinkles musically in the background. And the mountain is there, waiting impassively in the distance, and the *mesero* with his tray of iced drinks is perpetually poised just offstage. The Real Mexico...where the drink or the meal arrives hours after you've forgotten you ordered it, and the bus is always five hours late, or else there is no bus, but it doesn't matter. *No le hace.* It doesn't matter.

No le hace. That's the lesson you learn in Mexico. *No le hace.* It doesn't matter. Mexico, the Real Mexico, is a state of mind. You don't go to it. It comes to you. It's a matter of windage and elevation. It's a matter of adjusting your set. The Real Mexico is a state of mind in which you always have five hours until you catch the bus...

20

AS EASTER APPROACHED, Ysela pressed me to go to church for communion. I agreed, but her dates with Juan "El Indio" Mendoza were getting in the way. Why should I take communion with a whore who had no intention of being true to me? But my question was its own answer. Ysela *was* a whore. She had no obligation to be true to me or to any man. Her means of sustenance was the selling of her favors to men. I was one of many bees buzzing around a flower.

So I got off my high horse and agreed to go with her. It was all set. We attended Mass on Easter morning. I wore a suit and Ysela looked ravishing in a frothy white dress. It was her confirmation dress, she insisted, and I believed her. After all, it hadn't been all that long ago.

After we entered the dimly lit cathedral and took our seats, I felt a sense of peace. We really were a bride and groom now. The sordidness of the past was washed away and we were clean and new, a man and a woman, Adam and Eve again, and our union was pure and ordained by God.

The priest shook his censer; he muttered some words. The people—the seats were filled by now—responded, and so did Ysela. I didn't know what was required of me so I sat with my hands folded in an attitude of prayer. After some more rigmarole that I didn't understand, we started marching up to the altar, row by row, where we took the wafer and the chalice from the priest, the body and the blood of Christ. As we left the altar and the wine trickled down my gullet, I glanced at Ysela, walking beside me. I didn't know what to expect, but when our eyes met I sensed that, for the moment at least, our personal melodrama was jettisoned and we were archetypal beings marching to a timeless rhythm.

It was directly after this that we celebrated a sort of secular communion, Ysela and I, at the room. It was early morning. We were famished, and we were broke, too, since we'd spent what little money we had the night before on drinking. Waiting for us on the table by the window was a half-empty bottle of Misión de Santo Tomas *vino tinto* and a few stale tortillas from the Restaurant Palenque, already a little moldy around the edges. We sat down at our table and peered out the window at some drunken soldiers staggering along the bank of the green-water canal that flowed past *Calle Degollado* to the *Lago Blanco*, the White Lake Club. Farther north, a wooden plank bridge was thrown across the canal in front of the Hotel Roma. Here, at the Hotel Roma, on soldiers' payday night, laughing girls hung off the balcony, their hair awash, freely baring their breasts as an enticement to the passerby. In front of the Toluca Club, a few doors distant, the familiar beggar children were gathered, huddled together like frozen puppies as dawn came up like a house afire behind the red-tiled roofs and the church-steepled silhouette of the slumbering city.

I broke the spots of green mold off the stale tortillas, then, silently, Ysela and I drank the wine and ate the tortillas without salt. Then I threw Ysela down on the bed and twisted her arm behind her back. I drove my elbow into her chest and my knee into her thigh, crushing her body with the full weight of mine. At the same time I fucked her, I brutalized her. I knocked her bottom out while she bit my shoulder and chest and clawed deep furrows in my back and begged for more. She didn't want to come; she wanted to bleed. Her hunger for pain, for expiation, was boundless. It was as if she must answer in her person for centuries of evil deeds. She wanted subjugation beyond subjugation, pain beyond pain, she wanted to suffer as no one had ever suffered before.

When the former Brazilian Mirage III pilot arrived, she told me he was her brother. That took a lot of nerve. He was a fine specimen of a man, outrageously handsome, with cascading curls and flashing brown eyes. Clearly, I was outclassed. He shot me out of the sky with a single burst of his twin 30mm cannons. I could feel myself going into a tailspin...

Not only that, but I was about to get sick. Maybe that was my left-handed way of abdicating my impossible position. First we went to the Palmeras Club and *he* was there. He asked her to dance and I cut in. Later, back at the room, I gave Ysela a good smack in the face, then dragged her across the floor and shoved her against the wall and shook her. She struck back at me furiously, her eyes brimming with tears. I could tell she was pleased. I was finally becoming abusive. But my heart wasn't in it.

The last thing I ate was a bowl of vegetable soup at the Eagle Cafe. It was very near the site of the old Acme Saloon where Wes Hardin was gunned down in 1895. I began to feel deliciously weak and woozy. One thing I knew: I'd been handed a knockout punch. The rest is hazy. I paid my bill. I caught the *tranvia*. I made my woozy way to Juárez, instinctively heading for the Bottle Club, La Posada de Los Indios. I got the key from Ysela, who was on duty, and went up to the room. Later, after I'd been sleeping, I felt her slipping into bed beside me, cool as a glass of water. Then I saw her busying about, getting dressed, combing out her hair, waving goodbye, pulling the door shut behind her. After what seemed like a matter of minutes I heard a jingle of keys and she was slipping back into bed beside me.

Days and nights passed like this, I don't know how long. I heard voices in the street, horns honking, distant shouts of vendors hawking tamales and *helados*. And music coming from the Bottle Club down the block when the door swung open. And the parrot at the Toluca Club, two doors north. He kept rattling his cage and croaking, "You want a *weeskey*, Señor?" I couldn't help laughing. Maybe that's what happens when you die, I thought: an angel with green parrot wings comes flapping up to you and croaks, "You want a *weeskey*, Señor?"

I lay on the bed, my chest heaving with silent laughter, while tears trickled down my cheeks. Ysela came and sat beside me. "*Por qué tan triste?* Why so sad, my love? Ah, but you're laughing..."

Then I got the chills. I was freezing. I couldn't stop shivering. She piled blankets, clothes, sweaters, on top of me. Then she got into bed, naked, and hugged me with her arms and legs. We were two Eskimos huddled under our sealskins, voyaging in the Arctic night.

"You want a *weeskey*, Señor?"

Time was passing, hours, days...

Sometimes Ysela would come to my bedside and jokingly mimic the bird: "You want a *weeskey*, Señor?" Then she'd laugh, showing her dazzling white teeth. She was so beautiful, so warm. She'd sit on the edge of the bed. What was she doing? A crossword puzzle, or she seemed to be arranging some glass beads on a little card like a checkerboard. A game, or maybe she was sewing. I couldn't quite tell. "*Mi amor*," she'd whisper tenderly when she'd look up and catch me staring at her. Once she poured some water from the clay pitcher on the stand near the window and mixed something in a bowl. Then she sang a dreamy little lullaby. The words were strange. It wasn't Spanish or English. An Indian song, I decided. I watched her put a steaming pack on my chest. She made me swallow something from a cup. It was bitter. After I dozed off, I heard her humming to herself, that same dreamy lullaby.

Then paranoia gripped me. It took possession of my mind. That stuff in the cup: Was it tea—or a concoction of herbs? The Eagle Cafe, that bowl of soup... I hallucinated that. I was never sick. The medicine she gave me, the concoction she mixed in the bowl, what was it? *Yage?* Something more powerful, something unheard of? I was enchanted, drugged. I was a prisoner of Circe, the pig-mistress. Ysela was a sorceress, a powerful and inhuman *curandera.* Of course! Why hadn't I realized that before? I tried to fight back, but I couldn't even move my arms or legs, I was so weak. I was finished! Then I laughed. What did it matter now? It didn't. My discomfort was an event in the cosmos, a tiny electrical flare-up on the face of an immense blazing sun. It didn't matter. *I* didn't matter. The sun was shining and the current was flowing and I was floating down the river in an inner tube, headed for the Blessed Isles, for Zihuatenejo.

"You want a *weeskey,* Señor?"

Morning. I blinked my eyes. Something was different. The fever had gone. My mouth was dry; my tongue was thick and furry. I grabbed the clay pitcher from the rickety stand next to the bed, but the pitcher was empty. The room was empty.

Ysela...

I reached for my pants. I felt giddy, billowy. I went to the window and pulled back the curtains. It wasn't morning after all, I noticed. It was evening.

I went downstairs to the bar. Ysela was there, dancing with the Brazilian flier. Incredibly handsome, this man, with his thin cruel lips and his bomber jacket and his romantic dangling curls. Ysela was gazing into his eyes as they swayed to the music. I knew that look. It was the way she used to look at me. Poetic justice, I told myself. This ape-man, fresh from the banana jungles, he'll do what I can't do. He'll beat the shit out of her and then he'll give her the time. That's what she wants, what she needs.

Suddenly, I realized I was thirsty.

"*Agua*," I told the bartender.

"*Mande?*"

"Water!"

I drank three glasses of water in quick succession. I'd never been so thirsty in all my life.

"Water! More water!"

I drank ten glasses of water and threw a dollar bill down on the bar. The bartender gawked at me as if I were crazy. I felt wonderful...

A dozen years elapsed before I returned to Ciudad Juárez. I'd gone through a nasty divorce and had just returned from Europe with my fiancée, Gretchen, who had gone on to Pittsburgh to visit her mother, who was ill with cancer. Later, we met and were married in New York City, where, as we strolled the familiar streets, huge blocks of my childhood came back to me as vividly as if I were watching a film based on my life. But there was no time for reminiscing. Gretchen and I were off to Germany to visit her relatives and complete our honeymoon tour of the *Romantische Strasse*, which had been interrupted by the news of her mother's illness.

I checked into the Gateway Hotel in El Paso as night was falling. Of course I couldn't sleep, so I went for a walkabout in the sleet that was freezing on the sidewalks, slipping and sliding past the old haunts: Coney Island, Alligator Park, the Hollywood Cafe.

Next morning, bright and early, I was up and pounding the pavement in a howling blizzard. Four inches of snow had fallen during the night. Car roofs and store awnings were blanketed white, and kids were throwing snowballs.

On Mariscal Street, the air was crisp and cold. I didn't

feel like going into the clubs. Sometimes it's best to leave things as they are. It's like painting a picture: you have to know when to stop. It's important to embrace the world with open arms, to grapple with life, to pounce, to devour, to digest, but it's also important to know when not to enter the fray, but to withdraw, to abdicate, to simply pass by.

I opened the door of the Navy Rose Club and peered inside. Not one familiar face. Time had eroded Mariscal Street like a river. I sauntered along. The doors of the cantinas were flapping. An old woman emptying her slop bucket on the frozen earth looked up at me and grinned toothlessly.

The past is literature.

Back at my hotel room, I call Gretchen. No answer. Sitting on the edge of the bed, I write her a postcard. Stupid, in a way, because I'll be there before she gets it. The important thing is, tomorrow I'll be in New York. Tomorrow I'll be with Gretchen.

I fall peacefully asleep, and then I dream. I'm on Mariscal Street, in one of the cantinas. I enter a room, walking behind a woman. There's a rumpled bed, and a saint's candle flickering in a corner. I reach into my pocket and spread bills and coins out on the dirty bed sheet. The girl stands with her back to me, gazing out the window. Then she crosses her arms over her head and pulls off her dress. Meanwhile, instead of taking off my pants, I set up the machine gun I'm carrying. I snap open the tripod, stick one end of the belt into the breech, work the action to chamber a round and swing the gun up. Naked, surprised, smiling, she turns to face me and I stitch her up the front. The bullets shatter the windowpane behind her and ricochet off the walls of the buildings. The city is in flames. Sections of broken sky shear away, bursting like clay pigeons. Holding the trigger down, I chop it all to pieces, the fizzing neon lights, the tiny *loncherías*, the donkey carts, the ragged street dogs, the *Indios* on the road with their burdens...

Tomorrow, I will write about my childhood.

ABOUT THE AUTHOR

Donald O'Donovan was born in Cooperstown, New York. A teenage runaway, he rode freights and hitchhiked across America, served in the US Army with the 82nd Airborne Division, lived in Mexico, and worked at more than 200 occupations including telephone psychic, undertaker and roller skate repairman. A former long distance truck driver, he wrote *Confessions of a Bedbug Hauler* while running 48 states and Canada for Schneider National. As a volunteer at the Braille Institute in Los Angeles he recorded several western novels, and subsequently studied voice acting with James Alburger and Penny Abshire. O'Donovan lived for two years at the historic Wilshire Royale Hotel while writing *Tarantula Woman* (Open Books, 2011), and wrote the first draft of *Night Train* (Open Books, 2010) on 23 yellow legal pads while homeless in the streets of LA. An optioned screenwriter and voice actor with film and audio book credits, Donald O'Donovan lives mostly in Los Angeles.